Allie went very still, and she drew in a long, shaky breath. "Sam?"

"Yes." The fact she was glad it was him shouldn't have had the effect on him that it was.

"Oh, God, I thought you were a burglar."

And then she was snuggled against him, tears chasing down his bare, already wet, chest. It was his turn to go very still.

This, he realized, was going badly off the rails. Very badly.

"Obviously, this can't work," Sam informed her with elaborate patience. "You and me together under the same roof. I mean..." He waved a hand at her. "You can't wander around in your underwear."

"It's not my underwear," she said, dangerously. "It's a bathing suit."

"Dear God," he muttered under his breath.

She was the type of woman who would probably bring all kinds of unexpected surprises with her for a man foolish enough to tangle his life with hers.

Even for two weeks.

Allie glared at Sam. She had to remind herself where excitement could lead, and that she had already visited that place, with disastrous results.

Dear Reader,

I am one of those people who love summer. I can't seem to get enough of the colors, the sounds and the scents of long sunshine-filled days. As a Canadian, I know all too well about the cold, dark, dreary days of winter.

And so, when I was looking for a *feeling* for this book, I chose California. From my visits there, it seems to be a place of ceaseless summer, happy energy and exciting vibrancy.

Both Allie, the heroine of this story, and Sam, the hero, had experienced a kind of winter of the soul. I felt they needed carefree days against the backdrop of sun and sand, bonfires, and fireworks to thaw, to heal and to allow the warmth of love back into their lives.

So, in whatever season you are reading this book, my wish is that it transports you to the laughter-filled, revitalizing days of an endless summer.

With warmest wishes,

Cara Colter

Tempted by the Single Dad

—

Cara Colter

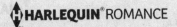

Recycling programs
for this product may
not exist in your area.

ISBN-13: 978-1-335-55610-3

Tempted by the Single Dad

First North American publication 2019

Copyright © 2019 by Cara Colter

This edition published by arrangement with Harlequin Books S.A.

For questions and comments about the quality of this book, please contact us at CustomerService@Harlequin.com.

® and TM are trademarks of Harlequin Enterprises Limited or its corporate affiliates. Trademarks indicated with ® are registered in the United States Patent and Trademark Office, the Canadian Intellectual Property Office and in other countries.

Printed in U.S.A.

Cara Colter shares her life in beautiful British Columbia, Canada, with her husband, nine horses and one small Pomeranian with a large attitude. She loves to hear from readers, and you can learn more about her and contact her through Facebook.

Books by Cara Colter

Harlequin Romance

A Crown by Christmas

Cinderella's Prince Under the Mistletoe

The Vineyards of Calanetti

Soldier, Hero...Husband?

The Gingerbread Girls

Snowflakes and Silver Linings

Battle for the Soldier's Heart
Snowed in at the Ranch
Second Chance with the Rebel
How to Melt a Frozen Heart
Rescued by the Millionaire
The Millionaire's Homecoming
Interview with a Tycoon
Meet Me Under the Mistletoe
The Pregnancy Secret
Housekeeper Under the Mistletoe
The Wedding Planner's Big Day
Swept into the Tycoon's World
Snowbound with the Single Dad
His Convenient Royal Bride

Visit the Author Profile page at Harlequin.com for more titles.

To the brother I found in my place of endless summer, Jeffrey Byron Werle.

Praise for
Cara Colter

CHAPTER ONE

IT WAS A perfect moment. Of course, if there was one thing Alicia Cook had a right to distrust, that was it. Perfect moments.

Still, with a sigh, and a sip of her lime-infused club soda, Allie gave herself over to it. The setting sun was gilding the foam on the ocean waves, and turning the beach sand to pure, luminous gold. From the hanging porch swing in the shadows of her covered veranda, she observed as the daytime crowds dissipated.

Now, one last family remained, the father deflating a humungous ride-on dragon water toy, the mother shaking out a picnic blanket and calling the children back from the water's edge as she packed the remains of their day into an oversize basket.

A pang of pure longing hovered at the edges of Allie's perfect moment, so she shifted her focus. Farther down the beach a couple strolled, hand in hand.

The sense of longing intensified.

"Don't believe a word he says," Allie muttered, watching through narrowed eyes as they stopped, leaned into each other and he nuzzled her ear and said something to her that made her laughter carry up the beach.

Allie's muttered words were a defense, of course, against all that weakness that was still there, even though she, of all people, should know better than to long for dangerous things.

Perfect moments. To not be alone. To share life. To be deeply connected…there, her perfect moment was gone. She looked away from the couple, ignored the family and took a determined sip of her drink, concentrating furiously on the beauty of the setting sun, hoping to get it back.

No, the moment had been as iridescent—and as fragile—as a soap bubble blown from a child's wand. It was gone.

She set down her drink, leaned over and drew her guitar from a shadowed corner.

"Perfect moments do not pay bills, anyway," Allie told herself sternly. The contract to produce a jingle was the practical approach to solving her financial difficulties.

The guitar, however, was unmoved by the urgency she felt. She ran her thumb coaxingly down the six strings—E, B, G, D, A, E—but the guitar refused to be seduced. The instrument was acting like a friend who was mad at her, silent, refusing to speak.

It was almost a relief—a reprieve—when Allie heard a muffled noise through the patio door that opened into the cottage behind her. What was that? Was someone at her front door? She strained her ears. That had to be her imagination.

The very same imagination that would not give her a song, was quite happy to indulge her fears, she noticed.

But as she strained to hear, she could have sworn the sound she was hearing was very real. She was hearing the creaky front door handle being tried!

A recent newspaper article had been pinned to the community bulletin board in front of the post office. Mimi Roberts's villa—located just down the beach—had experienced a break-in. An audacious thief had come in the front door while Mimi was home, but fortunately for the well-known celebrity, she was out back enjoying her deck. A Sugar Cone Beach police spokesman said there had been several similar break-ins in the neighborhoods surrounding the beach community and urged people to lock those front doors, even while they were at home.

Honestly, Allie had had trouble sleeping ever since, awaking to every sound, too hot because she was keeping the doors and windows firmly locked. No wonder she couldn't write a simple jingle. Sleep deprived.

A muffled *bang* made her jump. Okay. It was definitely her front door. Being kicked in? No, probably something way less threatening, like a newspaper being thrown up against it.

You don't get the paper, a little voice insisted on reminding her.

Still Allie tried to reason with herself. It would take an extraordinarily unambitious thief to choose her little cottage for break-and-enter purposes. The end of Sugar Cone Beach that was farthest away from her had long since gone to developers. High-end hotels and condos, with their main floor restaurants and shops, vied for every inch of space along that baby-powder-fine stretch of sand.

But the beachfront properties at this end of Sugar Cone Beach—a sheltered bay—were largely single-family homes that had become the enclave of the very wealthy, like Mimi Roberts. For the past twenty years extravagant beach houses had been popping up here. The glass, concrete and steel behemoths rose out of the sand on either side of Allie.

And there she sat, in the middle of them all,

in a sagging and tiny gray-shingled cottage, that had been her grandmother's for as long as she could remember.

Gram. Allie felt the ache in her throat that momentarily overrode the adrenaline that was beginning to pump through her. Her Gram was the one person who had stuck by her, believed in her and never given up on her.

Gram was gone now but the cottage that was so beloved to them both had been her final gift to Allie.

If Allie could hold on to it. The taxes alone took her breath away. And every day, someone came, ignored the unfriendly sign that said No Soliciting and knocked on her front door. They were developers and real estate agents, and people just passing by, putting temptation in front of her, offering her ridiculous sums of money to sell the one place in the world where Allie felt safe and hidden from prying eyes.

And where the love of her grandmother remained, as comforting as a hug.

There was definitely somebody at the door but Allie calmed herself with the rationale it was probably not a thief, though it was unlikely to be a real estate agent at this time of day, either. Whoever it was, they weren't ringing the bell.

The bell hasn't worked for three weeks, Allie told herself. *It's not a thief.*

But whoever it was, they weren't giving up, either.

Allie put down her guitar, not unaware that she felt relieved for a distraction, no matter how unpleasant that distraction might be. She got up, and went through the back into the cottage, not sure of the proper protocol for a would-be break-in.

Should she make lots of noise and throw on all the lights so it was apparent someone was home? Or should she tiptoe up to the door and peek out the front window?

Coming from the brightness outside into the cottage was like being plunged into a mine shaft. It had originally been a fisherman's place—the only one that remained on this stretch of beachfront. Back in the 1920s, when it was built, no thought at all was given to such frivolous concerns as where to place windows to take most advantage of the view. Windows would have been regarded as a luxury in those days.

And so the kitchen was in the back of the house, cramped and dark. Faucets dripped and cabinet doors hung crookedly, and the painted wooden floor was chipping. Despite all that, there was a determined cheeriness to the space, a laid-back beach vibe that Allie adored.

One summer she and her grandmother, in an attempt to brighten things up, had painted all the cabinets sunshine yellow, and they had liked the color so much they had done the kitchen table, too. They had installed a backsplash of handmade sea-themed tile, and hung home-made curtains with a pink flamingo motif.

Off the kitchen, there was a narrow hall, painted turquoise, with Allie's childhood art hung gallery style. There were three tiny bed-rooms on one side of the hall, each holding little more than a bed, a bureau and a night-stand. Her grandmother, a quilter, had loved fabric and every closet in the whole cottage was stuffed with it. Allie could not bring her-self to throw a single remnant away. Each bed was adorned with a handmade quilt. Allie's fa-vorite, the double wedding ring pattern, was on her own small bed.

Still tiptoeing, Allie followed the hallway to the front door, and the arched opening to the living room, where a paned picture window looked onto the street. The furniture and the wooden floors, worn to gray, sagged equally with age and good use.

In the heyday of her career—imagine being twenty-three years old and the heyday of your career was already over—Allie had been in many houses that looked like the ones on either side of her. Houses that were open plan, with light spilling in huge windows, and stainless steel appliances bigger than most restaurants required. They had miles of granite countertops, gorgeous beams and sleek furniture. Not one of them had ever made her feel this way.

Home.

That's what she needed to remember about the career that had soared like a shooting star, and then fizzled even more quickly, and that's what she needed to remember when another million-dollar offer was made. Neither success nor money could make you feel at home. She steeled herself to the possibility of temptation as she moved past the door to have a peek out the window.

But before she made it past, there was another thump. Someone *had* kicked the door! Her heart flew into double time. Then, to Allie's horror, the door creaked open an inch. Allie stopped and stared, her heart in her throat. Her first instinct, the one she had reasoned herself out of, had been correct.

Home invader.

She was sure she had locked the front door since seeing the news report.

Not that it mattered. Locked or not, her space was being invaded! Her safe place was being threatened.

In one motion, she reached out and grabbed the nearest thing she could lay hands on—a heavy statue, one of her grandmother's favorites. It was a bronze of a donkey, looking forlorn and unkempt. Weapon firmly in hand, Allie threw her weight against the opening door, trying to force it closed again.

Sam Walker was beyond exhaustion. He'd been late getting away. The traffic heading to the beaches of Southern California, in anticipation of the upcoming Fourth of July holiday, had been horrendous. And his traveling companions were cantankerous.

The key had been sticky, but finally worked. But despite trying to persuade it with his foot—twice—the door remained stuck.

He was used to the cottage being a touch temperamental, but his patience was at a breaking point. Sam had had quite enough of cantankerous *anything* for one day. The floorboard beneath the door was probably swollen with moisture or age. He'd put it—and the lock—on his list of things to fix while he was here. Not even in the door yet, and he had a list of things that needed doing. *Normal, mature man things. What a relief.*

The door had finally opened a miserly inch and then jammed stubbornly. Sam's patience broke. He put his shoulder against it and shoved, hard, two years on the college football offensive line finally put to good use.

The door flew open, and his momentum catapulted him through the opening. He was rendered blind by the sudden entrance into cool darkness, in sharp contrast to the outside, where the world was being washed with end-of-day light.

The hair on the back of his neck rose when he heard a startled grunt somewhere in the dark space in front of him. He squinted, his muscles bunching. Hadn't he seen on the news there had been break-ins along this stretch of beach?

Sure enough, there was the intruder. The force of the door opening had slammed him to the floor, where he lay, stunned, catching his breath. He didn't look immediately threatening—small, probably a teenager up to no good.

Casting one quick look at his cantankerous companions—thankfully, stuck in the yard—Sam thrust himself forward. He realized the kid, burglar, intruder, whatever, was starting to sit up. It appeared he had something in his hand to use as a weapon.

"What the hell do you think you're doing?" Sam asked, his voice a growl of pure threat. And then he lunged forward, easily won a tug-of-war for the object and tossed it aside. He pressed down on the kid's shoulder, hard, forcing him to sit, not rise.

The squeak of pain was sharp and, he registered slowly, *not* masculine. At all. A light, clean fragrance tickled his nostrils.

The momentum that had been propelling Sam forward came to a screeching halt.

His eyes adjusted to the lack of light. It wasn't a kid. And it wasn't a boy, either. Eyes as big as cornflowers, and nearly the same color, flashed up at him, filled with fury and indignation.

He let go of her shoulder instantly, but still, held up his hand, warning her not to get up.

It was the perfect ending, he thought wearily, to a perfectly awful day.

CHAPTER TWO

ALLIE PULLED HERSELF to sitting, feeling stunned and winded. She glared up at her attacker, filled with impotent fury mixed with panic. A stranger was in her house! Asking *her* what the hell she was doing! Ordering her, with imperious hand signals, to sit here, as if she was a prisoner!

Was she a prisoner? Her shoulder tingled oddly where he had touched it, and she resisted the urge to rub it, as if that would betray weakness.

As he folded his arms over the rather impressive contours of his chest, and planted his long legs, she felt, weirdly, as though her panic was put on pause. She had a sense of being caught in a luxurious place of slow time suspension as she studied him.

Surely home invaders did not look like this? She could see the man was very tall. The last bits of sun creeping over his extraordinarily broad shoulders spun his dark hair to milky chocolate. He looked strong and fit, and carried his body with that casual confidence she assigned to athletes, not to someone up to no good.

Allie saw the man was well dressed in pressed khaki shorts that made his bare legs look very long, and a sports shirt that hugged the enticing muscle of very masculine arms.

There could be worse people to take you prisoner.

She was appalled at this traitorous thought.

Of course he would look well dressed. That was exactly how a thief would try to blend in, as he was out trying door handles and breaking down doors in an upscale neighborhood like this one.

The intruder backed up from her, slowly, keeping his eyes on her, until his hand was on the doorknob.

Leaving, she deduced with relief.

But then he took his eyes off her for a moment, and glanced outside. It occurred to her he had a partner in crime, an accomplice.

Then she noticed keys dangling from the lock. How could she have been so stupid? She had locked the door, yes, but left the keys in it. The pressure to produce the jingle was making her absent-minded, obviously.

Allie weighed her options and saw two. He was distracted right now. She could get up and race back down that hallway, and out onto the beach before he knew what had happened.

She was rather shocked to discover her unwillingness to retreat. This was her *home*, her safe place. This was the one thing she had left that she was willing to make a stand for.

"Get out while you can," she ordered him. She staggered to her feet. She hoped her voice wasn't as wobbly as her legs were. Thankfully, she had lots of experience overcoming nerves, especially with her voice. She slipped her hand into her shorts pocket. "I have a weapon."

The part about a new weapon was a complete fib. Still, you would think he would have the decency to be startled at this latest threat to his diabolical plan, whatever it was.

But no, the man turned back to her, ever so slowly, and regarded her through narrowed eyes. With the last light spilling in the front door, she could see her home invader was one long, tall drink of handsome!

"I think we've already dispensed with the weapon," he said, something dry in his tone, almost as if he found her laughable.

"I have another one," she insisted, pressing her finger up against the shorts pocket in what she thought was probably a fair approximation of a pistol barrel.

He had chiseled, perfect features and eyes as dark brown as new-brewed coffee. His cheeks and chin were ever so faintly whisker-shadowed, but in a way that made him look roguish and sexy, not at all like the home invader that he was.

Allie was hoping, given her warning, he would bolt back out the way he came, but he didn't. He *frowned* at her, any amusement he felt at her efforts to defend herself completely gone.

He moved across the space that separated them in less time than it took her to take a single breath. He caught both her arms, tugged them out of her pockets, and pinned them to her sides. Her squirming to release herself only served to tighten his grip, so she stopped.

To her relief, it was apparent his hold on her arms was not intended to hurt, but to control. His touch was warm and made her pulse with a strange, electrical awareness of him.

It seemed to be an entirely inappropriate time to notice he smelled good, like a deep forest afternoon on a hot summer day.

Why hadn't she run when she had a chance?

"Who are you?" he asked, his voice an unsettling growl of something between menace and seduction. "And what have you done with Mavis?"

Shock shivered along Allie's spine. He knew her grandmother? He could have read her name on the mailbox.

No, he couldn't have. It had faded a long time ago. So, yes, he knew her grandmother. So what? Did that give him the right to barge into her house?

"What have *I* done with Mavis?" Allie stammered. She tried, again, to wiggle away from his grip, but he held her fast.

"Where is she?" He managed to say that as if Allie was barging into his home, and not the other way around.

"You think *I'm* the home invader?"

"You're the one with the pistol in your pocket."

She managed to wiggle her fingers just enough to reach into her pockets and turn them inside out. He looked unsurprised, and not impressed, at all. It was all too much. She had gone from panic to fury to this. Her life wasn't in danger. This was all some kind of misunderstanding.

Allie began to giggle. Okay, it might have had a tiny bit of a hysterical edge to it.

"I fail to see the humor," he said tightly. "It's been on the news. There have been break-ins in this neighborhood. Mavis would be very vulnerable."

She giggled harder. "I'm not the intruder. You're the intruder."

He let go of her shoulders completely, and looked down at her, his brow knit in consternation. "Who are you?"

"Who am I?" she sputtered. "I live here. I think the question is, who are you? And how dare you just walk into my home?"

"Your home?" The frown deepened around the exquisite corners of a wide mouth.

"I've rented this cottage from Mavis, in this time period, every year for the past ten years. My mom and dad rented it before that. That's why I have my own key."

What? Allie thought, completely taken off guard. She noted his voice was a masculine and sexy rasp. She could still feel her upper arms tingling from where he had held her fast.

Now that there was, obviously, no threat, her thoughts wandered. She despised herself for the wish that flitted through her mind: that her hair was not rumpled, towel-dried from her last swim, the tips still a shockingly different color than the rest of her blond hair. She wished she was not standing there, barefoot, in a too-large T-shirt that ended just past the shorts she had pulled on over a still-damp bathing suit.

Allie actually wished she had makeup on, which was totally against the cottage rules.

She snapped her mouth shut, since it had fallen open as she struggled to make the leap from home invader to well, home invader. Suddenly, it didn't seem very funny at all, and the giggle, hysterical or otherwise, died within her. He didn't know, and she hated being the one to break it to him.

"Mavis is my grandmother." Somehow, she couldn't bring herself to say *was* as if that would erase something too completely from her world. "She's gone."

"Your grandmother," he said, cocking his head at her, as if trying to discern truth.

"Yes, my grandmother."

Did he see some resemblance? People had always said she had her grandmother's eyes. They certainly shared a diminutive size. His shoulders suddenly relaxed. "Mavis goes every year. To visit her sister. But when I saw you here, it just shocked me. I wondered if she had come to harm."

"Do I look like the type of person who would harm an old lady?"

He looked at her carefully, as if he was weighing this. "You claimed you had a weapon in your pocket."

"When I thought I needed one for self-defense."

"You came at me with a lamp...or something."

"It's a statue, and I didn't exactly come at you."

"But you would have, if I hadn't knocked you over with the door."

Well, she couldn't deny that.

"That was an accident, by the way," he said, his voice both rough and soothing, "I thought the door was stuck so I threw my shoulder behind it. Are you okay? I didn't hurt you, did I?"

He must have decided she did not look like a mugger of old ladies, if he was interested, albeit reluctantly, in her well-being.

"I'll live."

He gazed at her steadily, as if trying to make up his mind, then rolled his shoulders, ran a hand through his hair.

"I apologize for acting as though you were an intruder. It's just that I was shocked to find you here. You're Allie, then. Allie of the artwork on the hallway walls. I guess I pictured Mavis's granddaughter as much younger. To match the artwork."

There was something vaguely unsettling about this stranger being familiar with the artwork of her younger self. Better to nip any familiarity in the bud.

"I'm sorry. I have some other shocking news. Mavis hasn't gone to visit my great-aunt Mildred. She—" But somehow, when she went to say the actual words, her lips quivered, and she could feel tears welling.

Talk about an emotional roller coaster! But maybe that is what shocks did to people? Put them through their whole range of emotions?

Understanding dawned in his face. "Mavis died?"

"Yes."

"I'm terribly sorry to hear that." He looked genuinely taken aback. He raked a hand through the dark silk of his hair again, and then glanced back outside.

Sorry. What an inadequate word. She made herself swallow back the tears that were forming and assume a businesslike tone. "I inherited the cottage. I wasn't aware of any rental arrangement."

"That explains being met at the door with—" he squinted over her shoulder "—a bludgeoning device."

"My grandmother called him Harold. The bludgeoning device."

"Is the fact that the bludgeoning device bears

a name supposed to make it more or less threatening?" he asked.

There was something about the faint smile that tickled the edges of that extraordinary mouth that made her feel just a little more off-kilter.

"As you said, there have been break-ins. I saw it on the news, too. Defense by Harold seemed like a good idea at the time."

"Look, you are about the size of a garden gnome…"

A garden gnome?

"…I don't think tackling an intruder head-on is the best idea. Harold or no Harold. The fake pistol in your pocket was really dumb."

Ouch. Not just a garden gnome, but a dumb garden gnome.

Allie had to get rid of him. She made her tone deliberately unfriendly. "I hardly need lectures from strangers."

"Not even a stranger you tried to bean with a sculpture?"

"Unsuccessfully," she muttered.

"I make my case." More softly, he said, "I don't feel as if we are exactly strangers."

The fact that he had seen her artwork did not make them friends.

"I liked your grandmother a great deal," he

said softly. "I think she would have wanted me to warn you against tackling intruders."

Allie did not like how his expression had softened with concern, as if she was a silly child who was in *need* of his supervision. Still, no point being churlish about it, especially since he was right: her grandmother would have approved of his well-meaning words.

"Well," Allie said, "thanks for your sage advice." Maybe the tiniest hint of sarcasm had gotten into her tone, because he was looking at her with his brows lowered in a most formidable way.

She would not be intimidated. "So, our mutual caring for my grandmother notwithstanding, I think our business here is concluded. Let me show you the door, Mr.…er…"

"Walker. Sam Walker."

"Mr. Walker, then. My apologies for the mixup. It will have left you in a bit of a pickle, but—"

"The pickle may be yours, I'm afraid. I have a contract."

CHAPTER THREE

ALLIE STARED AT Sam Walker, entirely flabber-
gasted by his arrogance.

The concern, along with his sympathy, had
evaporated. His tone suggested he felt that the
existence of a contract resolved everything. He
did, unfortunately, radiate a certain power, a
man very accustomed to obstacles melting before his considerable presence.

"I'm not sure what you think that means,"
Allie said, "that you have a contract. Or that
the pickle may be mine."

"It means, legally, I have possession of these
premises for the next two weeks."

"Are you a lawyer, then?" she asked, folding
her arms over her chest.

"No. But I have access to some pretty good
ones."

"Are you threatening me?"

"Not really."

But he was threatening her. Somehow this

threat felt more like a clear and present danger than him barging into her house.

"And what am I supposed to do?"

He lifted a shoulder, but seemed preoccupied with something he was looking at outside. "Vacate, I guess."

She didn't like this one bit: that in the blink of an eye she had gone from the one throwing him out, to the one being thrown! He was the kind of man who was like that: life-altering storms practically brewed in the air around him.

Vacate? Her own home? "You expect me to leave to accommodate you?" Her tone was properly indignant. And she hoped imperious.

He turned back to her. She got the impression that her indignation barely registered with him and that her leaving was exactly his expectation.

"I don't have anywhere to go," she sputtered. She sounded defensive. And faintly pathetic. Who didn't have anywhere to go? Plus, worst of all, she sounded as if she had already given up, as if she would defer to him and his stupid contract.

She had been so right not to trust that perfect moment of just minutes ago. Why did calamity lay in wait for her?

He lifted a shoulder and glanced back at her. "I don't, either. It's been a long day, and I'm not about to start searching for alternate accommodations now."

She could see, suddenly, that all that handsomeness had hidden a truth from her. His face was lined with weariness. And something else was in those devil-dark suede eyes...hurt? Loneliness?

Allie, she scolded herself, *you are in the middle of a crisis here.* She did not need to be exploring the damage to the dark stranger who had appeared on her doorstep.

And he did not want her to know, either, what painful secrets he held, because the window that weariness had opened briefly in his eyes slammed shut.

His voice had an edge of hardness to it when he spoke. "I couldn't find anything on such short notice, regardless."

That was true. It was the beginning of July. Sugar Cone Beach was one of the most sought-after holiday locations in California. People booked, particularly the July the Fourth holiday, well in advance. Sometimes, years in advance. People who had yearly arrangements—like him apparently—clung to them. She had heard of rental agreements being passed down, generation to generation, and that might be the case with him. He'd said his parents had it before him.

Still, it was even more reason she was not

abandoning her house to him. She would not be able to find anything else, either. Though the contract thing was a little worrisome. The last thing she needed was a legal battle. The truth was, after the shock of the tax bill, she was barely squeaking by.

Allie cast Sam a glance. He looked like he had a lot more money than her if it came to that.

Still, she couldn't act intimidated, and she couldn't take it on. It was his problem, not her problem.

"Who doesn't at least make a phone call before heading out on their holiday?" she asked, her tone querulous. "It's not as if my grandmother was young. Did it not occur to you things can change?"

He looked her over with narrowed eyes. His voice was cold when he spoke. "I happen to be one of the people most aware of how things can change, without warning, how an entire life can be thrown off course in a single second."

She was suddenly dangerously aware they were not talking about a rental agreement gone wrong. He looked stunned that he had revealed that much of himself, and covered his tracks quickly.

"We're going to have to reach an agreement," he said.

His tone was reasonable, but Allie could feel

herself bristling. Despite that lapse where he said a life could be thrown off course without warning—his life presumably—he was the kind of man who wouldn't like that. Who wouldn't like that one little bit. Who would move heaven and earth to make sure it didn't happen to him again. He practically oozed the kind of irritating confidence bordering on arrogance of a man who expected everything to go his way. Who would *make* everything go his way.

He was in for a surprise this time. He was going to have to go, and that was that. She was in creative mode—or trying desperately to be in creative mode—and she knew how easily the muse could be derailed. She had a deadline to meet. She had to stand as strong as him. This cottage was hers, and she was not leaving it!

"I doubt an agreement that is satisfactory to both of us is possible," she said.

"Thus the invention of contracts."

With his contracts and his annoying confidence, Allie decided she didn't like him at all. And that was a good thing. So much easier to make him go.

Wasn't possession nine-tenths of the law?

She opened her mouth to tell him—*Allie, show no weakness, particularly to a man like this*—but before she could say a single word, he was back out the door. The screen slapped shut behind him, and she went to see what had caught his attention so suddenly.

His keys still hung there. Maybe she could pull them out, slam the door and lock him out? She could imagine, with some satisfaction, the astonished look of disbelief that would bring to his unfairly handsome features.

Childish, she told herself, but in the face of his arrogance, his absolute certainty that he was right and she was wrong, she could not help but feel a certain glee at the prospect.

But when she moved to the front door fully intending to remove his keys, she saw what had pulled him out of her house with such urgency.

Allie's mouth fell open, her resolve evaporated and her heart dropped. Now what?

Just as Allie had first suspected, when she had seen Sam glance back out that door and hold it open, Allie's home invader had not arrived alone. No wonder, even as he spoke to her, he had been keeping a sharp eye on the front yard.

He was now crouched beside a small boy, who was trying to unstick a red wagon that had gone off the concrete pathway, and had its two side wheels imbedded in the soft dirt of the somewhat neglected flower bed that ran beside it.

The child was adorable: he looked to be maybe three, with a head full of tangled blond curls and the sturdy build of a tiny wrestler. Dimpled legs poked out of denim overall shorts. The chubby legs ended in tiny hiking boots. He had on a red T-shirt, and a faded superhero cape, one hem drooping, was draped over his shoulders and tied under his chin.

The wagon contained a small suitcase and a stuffed toy of some sort. The child was determined to free it himself.

He furiously waved off Sam, who could have freed the wagon in less than a second. Sam stood back, hands up, in the universal sign of surrender.

Allie realized it might be just a wee bit petty to take delight in seeing the self-assured Mr. Walker taking his orders from a child.

The little boy grunted and pulled, but the wagon did not move. But the stuffy did. It lifted its head, gazed with a combination of adoration and long-suffering at the child— an expression nearly identical to the man's, actually—then sighed, and put its head back down. Not a stuffy, then, but a dog. It looked like a cross between a cocker spaniel and a red feather duster.

Allie considered all of this. Finding accommodations would be hard enough in Sugar

Cone in July. The complication of the dog and the child would make it impossible.

Which meant what?

She could harden her heart to Sam Walker. It would take effort, of course, he was one of those men who effortlessly caused softening in the region of the female heart. However, she thought she'd become rather good at hardening her heart to men, and particularly one like him, who seemed altogether too sure of himself.

But the little boy? And that moppet of a dog?

What was she going to say? *Go sleep in your car? Go home where you came from? I don't care about you, or your excitement about a holiday on the beach?*

For all that she had been through, had she really become that person? Was she going to allow herself to be callous and hard?

It was a sensible approach to life, she tried to convince herself. She touched the ink-dark tips of her hair, as if to remind herself which way she needed to go if she did not want to be hurt any more.

But an attitude of complete cynicism did not feel as if it fit her, as much as she might have wanted it to. And her grandmother would not have approved.

Her grandmother had *known* this man. Possibly she had known him since he was a child.

She had never mentioned a rental arrangement, but Allie had never visited her at this particular time of the summer, either.

It occurred to Allie there might be a Mommy somewhere, but a quick glance at the curb showed no one else coming from the car that was parked there.

She couldn't identify the silver car, low-slung and sporty, beyond the fact that it was clearly *expensive*. The kind of car that a man who could afford a team of lawyers drove.

But then she thought of what she had glimpsed in the man's face, beyond the travel weariness, and it came to her. Not hurt, so much, and not loneliness.

It was a subject she was something of an expert on, enough that she could spot it in others. Loss. That is what was in the sharpness of his tone when he had told her that he, of all people, knew that life could turn on a hair.

Sam Walker knew some incredible, heart-breaking loss. That is what she had seen, naked in his eyes, before the veil had slammed down.

Of course, she probably had it all wrong. A divorce, plain and simple. In this day and age that would hardly cause a flicker. It was probably more the norm than not: marriage broken, daddy inheriting his kid for a week or two in the summer. What better plan than to head to the beach?

Allie sighed, and recognized it as a surrender. For tonight, anyway. She had two extra bedrooms. It was unlikely that a longtime tenant of her grandmother's had morphed into some kind of ax murderer. And also unlikely that an ax murderer came with a child and a puppy in tow.

Plus, there was the unhappy existence of a contract to consider.

Maybe there was a bright spot in all this. Maybe she needed to suck it up and consider going beyond tonight. Maybe, particularly since her guitar was locked into an unfathomable silence, Allie needed to consider giving up two weeks of her precious privacy in trade for something she needed more desperately than solitude right now.

Money.

Sam Walker sensed the girl had come outside behind him before he actually saw her. Awareness of her tingled along his spine, as she pressed by him, somehow not touching him, though the walkway was narrow. She paused at where the wagon was stuck.

"Hi," she said to Cody, who glanced at her, then ignored her.

She ignored him, too, none of that gushing over his curls that Cody and Sam were equally allergic to. Casually, barely seeming to move at all, she tucked her toe under the wagon, and lifted the stuck wheels back onto the walk. Sam noticed there was nary a protest from Cody, who trundled by her without acknowledging her help.

"I guess we can work something out," she said. Her voice was reluctant, but her eyes on the child had softened with a sympathy that turned them a shade of violet that Sam felt he could look at—or get lost in—for a long, long time.

He shook the feeling off, but still could not seem to stop looking at her. His initial reaction, in the poor light of the hallway, after he'd realized she was not a boy, had been that she was barely more than a child.

She had tufts of very short blond, sun-streaked hair—really sun-streaked, not from a bottle—in a rumple around her head. While the rest of her hair looked natural, there was an odd half inch, right at the tips, that was a disconcerting shade of black, as if it had been dipped in an inkwell.

She was wearing a too-long T-shirt, damp in the front, suggesting a swimming suit underneath it. She had very long, sun-browned legs, but otherwise was tiny, the kind of person who would be chosen for the part of Peter Pan in a play. Or maybe Tinkerbell. Despite being Cody's guardian for nearly eight months—all of them excruciating—Sam still wasn't really up on his children's stories.

Outside, the light dying, but better than it had been in the cottage, he could see she was not a child. At all. Maybe in her early twenties.

He could see, too, that she was the antithesis of the kind of women who populated his world. They fell into two categories: the very glamorous, with perfect makeup and salon hair, with manicured fingers and toes, and everything in between manicured, too. Those women wore designer clothes with casual flair, and tossed two-thousand-dollar handbags over gym-toned shoulders.

The other kind were his colleagues, professionals, as driven as he was, but as perfectly turned out as their glamourous counter parts, with a wardrobe of designer power suits and stylish eyeglasses.

Sam dated—occasionally—women from both those categories. Women sophisticated enough to understand that if they were looking for picket fences and happily-ever-after, he was not their guy.

But if they were looking for the kind of good

time—travel, posh restaurants, good wine, galas, charity balls, premieres—that money could buy, they could hang out with him. For a while. As long as there were no demands and they didn't get in the way of business.

This woman, with her blown-in-off-the-beach look, would not fit into either of those two convenient categories. He thought he had known women who were bold, but this woman who grabbed a statue named Harold and headed toward danger, instead of away from it, could redefine that word.

Next to any other woman he could think of she seemed, what? Distressingly real, somehow.

Not that categories for any kind of woman existed in his life anymore, Sam reminded himself.

No, his old life, that guy who worked hard and played harder, who was carefree and unfettered, was a distant memory, eight months behind him.

"Is there something wrong?" Ally asked.

On the other hand, maybe he would be getting his old life back soon. It was what he had wanted and wished for, almost on a daily basis.

And yet now that it was a possibility…his heart did a sickening fall.

CHAPTER FOUR

"Is something wrong?" she asked again.

He gave Allie of the hallway art—and possibly his landlady—a look. This was the second time he'd gotten the unsettling feeling that she might see things about him that others didn't. No one but his sister had ever seen past what he was prepared to show them, and he didn't like it.

But then he saw she wasn't even looking at him. She was looking at the dog, Popsy, lying in the wagon, one paw trailing, looking as boneless as a pile of rags.

"With the dog?" she clarified.

Sam felt huge relief that she was talking about the dog, not him.

Cody was now facing the challenge of the steps leading up to the cottage. With huge effort, he lifted the limp Popsy off the wagon. The dog reluctantly found its legs.

"Not permanently," he said and hoped that

was true. The dog was unusually attached to Cody. The two were inseparable. He did not think his sudden cosmically ordained family unit of uncle and nephew and dog could sustain another loss. And yet he didn't feel quite ready to tell her what the vet had said.

The dog is depressed.

Who knew that dogs got depressed? Or that little kids gave up speaking when the unspeakable happened to them?

"I thought I caught a whiff of something as they went by," she said, trying to word it delicately.

"The dog got carsick."

"Oh, no!"

Her sympathy was so genuine that he couldn't resist sharing the full horror. "You have no idea. At sixty-five miles per hour, with wall-to-wall traffic and not a rest stop for thirty miles. Then, when I finally could pull over, I had to unpack the suitcase to find new clothes. Not the Superman cape, though. I don't have an extra one of those.

"And guess how long the new clothes lasted before Popsy got sick on Cody again? I may never get the smell out of my car. Sheesh. I may never get the smell out of Popsy."

He stopped himself, embarrassed. He sounded just like those moms at the playgroup the counselor had recommended for Cody. Sam had tried to drop Cody off there several times.

Nobody warned me it was going to be this hard.

Cody, to Sam's consternation—he was trying to do the right thing, after all—and his guilty and secret relief, had used his limited communication skills to make it known he *hated* the play group.

"Cody is your son and the dog is Popsy?"

"Cody is my nephew, but yeah, that's the whole cast of characters."

Sam really hated sympathy, which made his recounting of the horrible trip down here even more mystifying. Still, right now, that sympathy—the soft look on her face as her gaze followed Cody and Popsy as they went up the stairs—served Sam well. He was seeing a whole shift in attitude.

"You must all be exhausted. I'll show you which rooms to take, and put out some towels. I'm sorry for the welcome I gave you earlier."

"Not your fault," he said gruffly.

"Well, let's start again. I'm Alicia Cook. Welcome to Soul's Retreat."

She held out her hand. Maybe it was a mistake to take it, because any sense he had left of her being a child disappeared in her grip. Her touch made him look at her differently. She was extraordinarily feminine, and her hand held the unconscious sensuality of the sea in it.

She was very pretty, her bone structure exquisite, her eyes a shade of blue bordering on violet that he would not have been able to name if asked. He was aware of a scent tickling his nostrils, and realized she smelled of the sea and something else. Lemons? Whatever it was, it was faintly ordinary and faintly exotic and faintly enticing.

It occurred to him that she had welcomed them as if she planned to be their hostess. Maybe that's why sympathy was not a workable strategy. Shared accommodations weren't going to work, and he needed to let her know right away. It looked like when she got an idea in that head of hers it was hard to displace it!

"I hope you won't have too much difficulty finding a place to stay," he said, and heard the cool, no-nonsense tone he used when closing a deal for his computer systems company.

All of it—especially the *enticing* part—made getting rid of her seem imperative.

That tone he had just used could—and had—intimidated business tycoons with global reputations. But her mouth—plump and pink—set in a very unflattering line, and her brows lowered.

"I'm not going to find a place to stay," she

said firmly. "Your arrival has taken me completely by surprise, but I'll accommodate you and Cody to the best of my ability tonight. Tomorrow we'll look at options. Maybe it will be workable for you to stay. With me."

"You want to share accommodations?" he asked her slowly. "With someone you don't know?"

"*Want to* seems to be overstating it a bit. None of you looks dangerous. The dog doesn't even look like it has the energy to bite."

Sam felt this odd little niggle, for the second time, of wanting to be protective of her.

Just as when she said she had a weapon when it was so pathetically obvious not only that she didn't, but that she wouldn't use it if she did.

Are you crazy? You don't invite strangers to stay with you.

But he managed to bite his tongue. He looked at the set of her jaw and felt a sudden exhaustion. It had been a horrible day. That *look* on her face felt as if it would take a lot more energy than he had to sort this out right now.

He needed to get Cody into the bathtub and into a bed. He had dealt with three of Cody's legendary meltdowns today. For a kid who didn't talk he was an absolute master at making his displeasure known to all. Sam was not up to another one any more than he was up to dealing with whatever the stubborn set of Alicia Cook's little mouth meant.

She was right. Tomorrow, they would look at options. Tomorrow, he'd deal with it. His team of lawyers could let her know he had an iron-clad contract and she could find someplace else to stay for two weeks.

He knew, despite a team of people working for him, that another place on Sugar Cone was out of the question for either himself and Cody or Mavis's granddaughter. They'd had a devil of a time finding a condo on the busier side of the beach for Cody's Australian auntie and uncle and their kids, arriving later in the week.

We need to know him better. He's all we have left of Adam.

Sam had met them, of course. At the wedding, the christening, Christmas two years ago. At the funeral. Good people. Decent. Hard-working. Real, somehow, in the same category that the woman in front of him was real.

And yet, when he thought of meeting them this time, he could feel his heart sinking to the bottom of his feet.

Despite the fact he was pretty sure he was botching nearly every single thing about raising a three-year-old, just like Cody was what they had left of Adam, he was what Sam had left of his sister, Sue, too.

And Sam had a history with this little cottage. He had been coming here for a long time. He had memories of endless days of him and Sue running on that beach as children. He desperately wanted Cody to feel the kind of unfettered joy that they had felt here.

Sam's parents had let the lease lapse when he and Sue were teenagers, but when they died, he had approached Mavis and asked about the possibility of leasing again. She, he remembered, had been delighted, almost as if she was waiting for him to come back. Since then, the cottage had always provided exactly what the sign, swinging at the gate with letters so faded you could barely read them, promised.

Soul's Retreat. Sam Walker was counting on this place to give him something that was in very short supply in his life right now.

Serenity.

Wisdom.

Wasn't there a prayer about those things? Not that he was a praying kind of man, though given the desperation of the decision he had come here to make, he wasn't going to rule out the possibility of becoming one.

What he didn't need were any further complications to a life that was seriously complicated right now.

And this woman, Alicia—Allie—with her

black-tipped hair, and a tiny bit self-conscious in her wet, too-large T-shirt, and trying hard not to let it show, had *complication* written all over her.

He was sympathetic about her grandmother. Of course he was. But, after tonight, she couldn't stay here with him under the same roof.

She looked like she was still the artsy type that her hallway art indicated. She'd probably love to go to Paris for two weeks. There. Problem solved. He would offer her a round-trip, all-expenses-paid to Paris so he and Cody could have the cottage to themselves.

If only all of life's problems were so easy to solve.

His more immediate problem was this: he had a very stinky dog and a very stinky kid on his hands. Neither of them liked baths.

"You've eaten, right?" Alicia asked, as she watched the shocking change in her life unfold before her very eyes.

Sam Walker stood in the bedroom she had suggested for Cody. The bedroom was not large, at the best of times, but now it looked positively tiny. Sam's shoulders seemed to be taking up all the space. He was rummaging through the small suitcase Cody had dragged up the walk on his wagon.

Cody and the dog peeked out at her from under the bed. The man and the boy had identical eyes, large, dark brown and soft as suede. There was something in them that could weave a spell around the unwary.

Which she was not.

"Yeah, we stopped at Pizza Palooza," Sam said, his voice a growl of unconscious sensuality. "Perfect Pal Happy Deals all the way around. Did they make me happy? No. I'm pretty sure that's what the dog threw up. I wonder if I can sue for misleading advertising?"

Allie felt a jab of sympathy for him. She reminded herself to be wary of spells, and overrode the sympathy. Much more sensible to see this as a reminder that he had a team of lawyers at his fingertips, and presumably, he was not afraid to use them.

Still, she had to venture, "I don't think the Perfect Pal Happy Deals are dog-designated."

"Did you hear that, Cody? The Happy Deal is not dog-designated. No more feeding Perfect Pal to Popsy. So, how about a bath, buddy?"

Sam had extracted a pair of pajamas from the suitcase. They looked as if they would fit a good-size teddy bear, and they had fire engines on them. Allie was finding this level of adorable invading her home doing very odd things to her heart, wary as it was.

The dog and the little boy shrank back a little farther under the bed. The man shot her a look, then got on his knees, rear in the air—and a very nice rear, at that—and looked under the bed.

"Come on," he said, his tone soothing, despite the exasperation Allie had so clearly seen on his features.

The boy scooted right out of sight. The dog made a sound that wasn't quite a growl, more like a hum of dismay.

Allie backed out of the room to leave Sam to his challenges, which seemed substantial. She reluctantly closed the open patio door—a precaution against the possibility of a burglar in the neighborhood. She was aware she felt a little safer with Sam in the house, though this reliance on a man to feel safe made her annoyed with herself.

Allie retreated to her bedroom, taking her tablet and her guitar with her. The bedroom proved not to be any kind of retreat at all.

For one thing, the cottage, with the closed patio door, was hot, her tiny bedroom window open a tiny burglar-proof crack, was not providing much of a breeze. She would normally leave her bedroom door open, but with guests in the house, that wasn't possible, especially since, as a defense against the suffocating heat, she stripped down to the bathing suit that was under her clothes. She appreciated its tininess, as much of her skin as possible exposed to the stingy breeze coming in her window.

She picked up her guitar and strummed it hopefully with her thumb, but it told her, with a certain sullen stubbornness, *no.* Which was too bad, because it might have covered the other sounds coming through the paper-thin walls of the cottage.

While she listened, the child was snared, a bath was run, the little boy splashing while his uncle made motor boat sounds.

There was something about Sam—so confident and so handsome—making motorboat sounds that made him all too human. He was a man way out of his element. And yet trying, valiantly, to do the right thing.

At some point Allie realized the little boy was not speaking, and it distressed her and made her realize she had not asked enough questions before allowing this pair, plus a dog, to share her home.

Why was she assuming Sam was doing the right thing? How did an uncle and nephew end up together on holidays? Why wasn't the little boy speaking? Where were the mommy and daddy? Was Sam Walker really the child's uncle? What if she had inadvertently embroiled herself in a parental kidnapping of some sort?

Though honestly, Sam didn't look like he was enjoying the exercise in child-rearing enough to have used illegal means to experience it.

Sam Walker did not look like a kidnapper any more than he looked like a home invader. In fact, he looked the furthest thing from a man capable of any kind of subterfuge. There was something in his eyes, in the set of his mouth, in the way he carried himself—in the way he handled the child and dog—that made him seem like a man you could trust, even if you didn't particularly like him.

Her grandmother had known him, she reminded herself. Had not just known him, but liked him enough to share an ongoing rental relationship with him for many years.

Still, Allie was aware that not only was she not sure what the *type* who became involved in a parental abduction would look like, but that she had an unfortunate history of placing her trust in people who had not earned it. While other people could trust their instincts, she had ample and quite recent proof that she could not.

Determined to not be naive, she put on her headphones to block out the noises coming from the bathroom and typed Sam Walker into the search engine on her tablet. Not too surprisingly, there were thousands of Sam Walkers. She changed tack and put in "recent abductions." Also, sadly, way too many of them, though no photos of a curly-headed little boy who looked like Cody. No abducted children *with* dogs.

Giving up, Allie Googled the legal ramifications of rental contracts, only to find out lawyers were quite cagey about dispensing free information over the internet.

After that, she went through her grandmother's documents, stored in a box under Allie's bed, hoping for the rental contract, but found nothing.

Through the headphones, she heard the muffled sounds of the bath ending. She took them off and listened.

The bed in the room next to her creaked, a small creak, and then a larger one. Too easy to picture.

"Get off, Popsy, you stink. And you're next for the bath. Don't even think of hiding. Okay, where is *Woozer, Wizzle, Wobble*? Here it is."

One bedtime story, read three times.

Again, that deep, sure voice, sliding over those silly words was all too endearing: "'And then the witch said, woozer, wizzle, wobble and turned the toad into a donkey.'"

Ashamed to realize that she was acting like

an eavesdropper and that the little scene playing out in the bedroom made her ache with that
same weak longing the family on the beach had
caused in her earlier, Allie put the headphones
back on. She turned the music up.

She pointed her finger at her silent guitar.
You are not my only source of music.

Then, she stretched out on her bed, and let
the faint breeze play over her skin. Without any
warning, the three nights of not sleeping suddenly caught up with her.

CHAPTER FIVE

CODY FELL ASLEEP before Sam had finished the third reading of *Woozer, Wizzle, Wobble*. He knew better than to stop. His nephew could rise out of a deep sleep, his neck swiveling like he was trying out for a part on an exorcism film, if he thought he'd been cheated of the entire third reading of his favorite book. For a kid who had given up on talking, Cody was remarkably adept at making his thoughts—particularly displeasure—more than apparent.

Sam finished the book, then slid out of the bed. Carefully, he undid the string that fastened the superhero cape around Cody's neck. A tender protectiveness for his nephew rose up in him, but it was followed with brutal swiftness by his awareness that when it had mattered, he had not been able to protect Cody at all.

As happened sometimes, the memory hit him without warning. His brother-in-law, Adam, laughing, as he and Sam chased after a shrieking Cody trying to get the cape off him for Sue to put in the laundry. Cody, fresh out of the bath, had been naked, save for the cape.

The dog had been there, racing joyously beside them, as they went in circles around the house, out into the yard, back into the house. Popsy had no idea what the game was, but loved it, nonetheless. They all had. Sue had pretended disapproval, but snickered anyway, when he and Adam had finally captured Cody and dubbed his garb "the Pooperman cape," a name that stuck.

What Sam hated the most was at the time he'd had no idea—none—how precious those moments were.

What he hated the most? Was that he had no idea if it—spontaneous joy—ever would come back. For any of them left living.

He was exhausted—which was probably why the uninvited memory had snuck in—but the dog was going to stink up the whole house if he didn't look after it.

He peered under the bed.

Popsy stared back at him, the picture of innocence. His face clearly said *What smell?* Sam made a swipe for him, and missed, which made Popsy retreat farther under the bed. Naturally, the dog made him crawl all the way under. At least he didn't growl—he saved that for when he was protecting Cody from the horrors of bath time. When Sam finally did manage to get him out and had him pinned in his arms, the dog trembled. Then he whimpered, a high, squeaking sound akin to the wire on a barb wire fence being tightened.

"Shhh," Sam told him, nudging open the bedroom door with his foot, "you'll wake Cody up." But what he was really thinking was *She's going to think I torture you.*

He stepped out into the hall. The house was dark and silent. Her bedroom door was firmly shut and no light came out from under it.

He tiptoed down to the bathroom. He had kept Cody's bathwater, and he slid the dog in. The dog yelped and squirmed, so with a deft motion, still hanging on to the dog, Sam managed to get his shirt off before he ended up completely soaked.

"This isn't my first rodeo," he informed the dog, who scrabbled to get out of the tub and, as he had predicted, totally soaked him within seconds.

He managed to keep hold of Popsy. The smell intensified—wet dog and vomit—as the water saturated the dog's fur. Sam reached for Cody's baby shampoo, somehow managing to hold the dog and dispense shampoo at the same time.

He lathered up the dog. Popsy resigned himself, giving a good demonstration of where the expression "hangdog" came from. Soon, the sweet smell of the baby shampoo began to smother the more noxious odors.

Sam splashed up water to get the lather off, and realized he was going to have to let the old water out of the tub to do a proper rinse. His guard went down ever so slightly and in a flash, the dog leaped out of the tub, nudged open the bathroom door and flew down the hallway, leaving a trail of water and soap in his wake.

Popsy burst through Allie's closed bedroom door, with Sam hot on his heels. In the murky darkness, Sam watched as the dog leaped onto the bed, landing with a squish on a rather delectable female body, lying on top of the covers. Even in the bad light Sam could tell she was wearing, well, next to nothing.

A pair of headphones and red bikini underwear.

Allie woke up flailing, her eyes wild with fear.

"Get away from me!" she screamed, throwing off the headphones, sitting up and swatting at the air. Popsy stayed on the bed but backed into the corner behind her, cowering.

Given the possibility she had a Harold nearby, or a suitable substitute, there was no explaining what Sam did next.

He moved slowly into the room, and sat down on the bed beside her. "I'm so sorry," he said in a low, soothing voice. "I was giving the dog a bath, and he broke away from me. I don't know how he got in your room. Maybe the door doesn't latch properly?"

She went very still, the screeching stopped, and she drew in a long, shaky breath. "Sam?"

"Yes." The fact she was glad it was him shouldn't be having the effect on him that it was.

"Oh, God, I thought you were the burglar."

And then she snuggled against him, tears chasing down his bare, already wet, chest. It was his turn to go very still.

He was nearly naked, and she was nearly naked.

And not at all in the way a man and a woman were usually nearly naked together. It shouldn't have felt as good as it did, and yet somehow, he could feel himself leaning into the warmth and suppleness of her skin. He recognized the closeness, the human contact, was pushing away some of the despair his memory had caused him just moments ago.

Thankfully, the romantic picture was completely interrupted by the sopping, soapy dog deciding to insert itself between them.

She laughed, a little of that shakiness still in her.

Against his better judgment, ignoring the wet puddle of dog, he stroked the short, spiky tufts of Allie's hair, and found them surprisingly silky. Allie softened more against him. The smell of her hair and the wet dog mingled, and somehow was not as unpleasant as it should have been.

This, he realized, was going badly off the rails. Very badly.

"How would you like to go to Paris?" he asked.

"Okay, if I wasn't certain I was dreaming before, now I am."

"No, I'm serious. Two weeks, all expenses paid. Paris." He moved an inch away from her. It took all his strength. Should it have taken so much strength? She was his landlady. He barely knew her.

"Paris," she said, her tone bemused, maybe even irritated.

He stood up, turned back, and faced her. "You could leave in the morning."

"I'm not following," she said. She didn't sound the way he had hoped she would sound. Which was happy. Who wasn't happy when they got an all-expense-paid trip to an exotic location?

"Obviously, this can't work," Sam informed her with elaborate patience.

She folded her arms around the wet dog, thankfully hiding most of herself, and looked at him with those eyes that could make a strong man weak. "What can't work?"

"You and me together under the same roof. I mean…" He waved a hand at her. "You can't wander around in your underwear."

"It's not my underwear," she said dangerously. "It's a bathing suit."

"Dear God," he muttered under his breath, trying not to be a complete pervert. That meant overriding his desire to look and see what the differences were between the underwear he thought it was and the bathing suit she proclaimed it to be.

"And I was not *wandering* around in it. You barged into my bedroom."

"Popsy," he corrected, weakly. "And the latch. Not working."

She went on as if he hadn't made those important clarifications. "Though it's a *bathing suit* and I live on a beach so it would be perfectly okay if I was wandering around in it."

Yes, indeed it would. It would be perfectly okay. For her to be prancing—wandering—around her own beachside cottage in a bathing suit. The fact that it was perfectly okay made it more of a problem, not less of one.

For him. A normal hot-blooded male.

That thought gave him pause. He had not thought of himself as normal for a long time. And hot-blooded had not been part of his equation since the accident had taken the lives of his sister and brother-in-law and plunged him into the familiar land of grief and the foreign one of parenting.

Is this how it would happen? Little normal moments would just insert themselves in his life when he was least expecting them? Not that this was a normal moment. Of course it wasn't. And yet, still, for one heady second, he had been dealing with a very normal, hot-blooded reaction to a woman.

Was he ready for that?

He didn't think so. She was the type of woman who would probably bring all kinds of unexpected surprises with her for a man foolish enough to tangle his life with hers.

Even ever so briefly.

Even for two weeks.

Besides, he had Adam's family arriving soon. What would they think about him co-habitating with a young lady given to skimpy red bathing suits? Surely they wouldn't think that was good for Cody?

No, he had to convince her to go to Paris. It felt as if his life—or what was left of it—might depend on that.

* * *

Allie glared at Adam. Paris, indeed!

Of all the places he could mention, did it have to be that one? Her ex-beau, Ryan, had whispered in her ear once, *We will explore the world together, and I will kiss you in Paris and my kisses will taste sweeter than wine...*

She shook away the memory, focused on something else. She was not in her underwear!

"Come on, Popsy," she said, getting up off the bed, and taking the dog firmly by the collar. "Let's get that soap off you."

The truth was, she was quite self-conscious in her red bikini. And a little bit pleased with the effect it was having on Sam, too!

He looked pretty stunning himself: his chest bare and wet, his shorts, also soaked, hanging low off slender hips. He was making her bedroom feel claustrophobic, just as he had Cody's.

Just moments ago, she had been cuddled up to him. Her skin was still tingling from it. How was she going to cleanse that memory from the room?

She could throw on a robe, but it felt as if that would be an admission he might be right about the wisdom of them sharing close quarters. It felt imperative not to let Sam win, somehow. Plus, she was going to be spraying off a dog.

How much sense did it make to get dressed for that activity? She pushed by Sam.

"But you haven't given me an answer about Paris."

When her day had started this morning, Allie could not have predicted any of its events, and certainly not for it to end with this kind of surprise: finding herself in the arms of a gorgeous man...who apparently would prefer her in Paris!

In fact, in her wildest dreams she could not have pictured any of this. There was something oddly invigorating about it all. In her attempts to make her life stable, and predictable, had it somehow teetered over an edge into boring?

On the other hand, she had to remember that playing with fire might also be considered invigorating. She had to remind herself where *excitement* could lead, and that she had already visited that place, with disastrous results.

"I'm *never* going to Paris," she told Sam firmly. "You are being ridiculous."

She glanced back at him. His brow was furrowed. People did not tell him he was being ridiculous, apparently.

Leaving Sam standing there, clearly stunned by her refusal, she took the dog out the patio doors, and down into a small fenced yard, where a hose was hooked up. It had a spray nozzle on the end. Popsy twisted her wrist trying to squirm out of her grasp.

"I thought cocker spaniels were water dogs?" she scolded him.

"Here. I'll hold him, you spray."

Sam had followed her outside and came down the stairs. He had put a shirt on. It felt like a reprimand.

He took the dog firmly in grasp while she hosed him off. The first time she squirted Sam instead of the dog, it was an accident. But the second time, it wasn't. Really? Who put on a shirt to wash a dog? And the third time it was pure devilment.

Of course, it was all fun and games until he grabbed the hose from her!

Given the heat of the night, the cold water hitting her did not have the effect she suspected he had hoped for. There was no cowering, no pleading for him to stop. The water felt delicious. She opened her arms to it, and tilted back her head and closed her eyes. The water stopped hitting her. She opened her eyes to see the stars studding an ink-black sky.

She lowered her gaze to earth. The hose had been set down. Sam was retreating, Popsy's collar firmly in his grasp. He stood, for one moment, at the sliding door, looking down from the deck at her.

From here, his eyes looked darker than the night sky.

And then Allie was in the empty yard alone, soaked, her very skin tingling with an awareness of life that she had not allowed herself to feel for a very, very long time.

She was aware she did not feel afraid of a burglar. For the first time in forever, she didn't feel afraid of anything, at all.

When she went in the house, she left the patio door wide open, so the breeze could cool off everything that had overheated this night.

Sometime during the night, her bedroom door creaked open, and she woke up, not to see the burglar the open door might have invited, but Popsy. The dog shuffled in, sniffed her hand and whined. The smell of baby shampoo barely masked the wet fur smell.

"What do you want?" Allie whispered.

The dog took that as an invitation. He put both front paws on her bed, hefted himself up and then snuggled his still-damp and somewhat smelly self into her side. He licked her cheek once, burrowed deep under her armpit and fell fast asleep.

She lay there for a moment, contemplating the rise and fall of his breath, and his uncomplicated affection for her. Maybe she needed a dog.

In the morning when Allie woke up, the dog was gone, but his scent lingered. She felt a bit cranky, almost like she'd had too much to drink the night before. The moment when she had felt so free and alive—in her drenched bathing suit under a star-studded night—now felt overlaid with embarrassment.

Allie forced herself to go for her normal early morning run along the beach.

If the trials of the past few years had taught her anything, it was that there was value in discipline and routine.

In a moment of weakness—thinking of the child, not the other set of deep brown eyes—she went as far as Mrs. Jacobs's Beachfront Bakery and bought half a dozen world-famous—according to Mrs. Jacobs—Sugar Cone muffins. They were hideously expensive.

Worth it, a half hour later, seeing the little boy, adorable in those pajamas with red fire engines all over them, and his hair an untamed tangle, chomping enthusiastically on his muffin, dropping crumbs to the dog. Popsy looked shiny and alert this morning. There were even signs of enthusiasm in the way he was noisily vacuuming Cody's offerings from the floor.

"Let's talk about Paris," Sam said.

He hadn't even said good morning. Or thanked her for providing breakfast.

CHAPTER SIX

"PARIS," ALLIE REPEATED, and slid Sam an incredulous look. "I thought I made it pretty clear last night how I felt about that idea."

"But that was before you had a chance to sleep on it." He smiled at her.

That smile made the sun, already drenching the kitchen, seem to shine more brightly. Sam Walker looked rather amazing in the morning. His teeth were straight and white and perfect, and when he smiled one side of his mouth lifted up more than the other.

He was also totally sure of himself in the tight confines of the kitchen, as if he wore pajama bottoms and bare feet in front of women all the time. Which seemed likely.

The plaid pajama bottoms hung low on slender hips, and his T-shirt hinted he might have participated in an Ironman or some other equally challenging display of masculine agility and strength.

She, on the other hand, had made a choice to cover herself up this morning, and was wearing ugly sweatpants and a shapeless T-shirt. Her hair was sweat-slicked.

His dark hair was also slicked, but in a much more attractive way.

Obviously he had showered. He had not shaved and his whiskers were even darker on his chin and cheeks this morning. It was a criminally sexy look.

She could tell he was used to being both charming and criminally sexy.

But something about all that charm was not reaching his eyes and it grated on her that he was used to getting his way because he had become adept at turning on the charm and throwing around some money.

"I am never going to Paris," she said, trying not to clench her teeth.

"Now *you* are being ridiculous. Everyone wants to go to Paris, someday. I can recommend a little café—"

Of course he could recommend a little café. He was obviously a citizen of the world, unlike her, a gauche girl from a small town who would fall for anything. Who had fallen and fallen hard. *We will explore the world together, and I will kiss you in Paris and my kisses will taste sweeter than wine...*

It made her stronger in the face of his considerable charm. "Mr. Walker—"

"I think we're well past that kind of formality," he insisted charmingly. She actually blushed, thinking of cuddling against him, and then doing her version of *Flashdance* under the stars.

She couldn't let that memory make her weak when she needed to be strong.

"I am not going anywhere," Allie said with all the firmness and sternness she could muster. She sounded like a schoolmarm speaking to an unruly boy. "I am not making a choice."

"But—"

"No! You obviously have a great deal of money you don't mind throwing around, so you go. I ran by a place for sale this morning. Go buy it."

He squinted at her with patent disbelief. The smile faded.

"I have the contract," he said.

"I don't care. I looked on the internet last night. It's debatable whether I have to honor a contract you signed with a deceased person." It hurt, more than she expected, to think of her Gram as a deceased person.

Thankfully, Sam didn't pick up on her sudden feeling of weakness. "You're taking legal advice off the internet?"

She folded her arms over her chest. Under normal circumstances, she might consider what he was offering.

After all, Paris! Maybe it would be exactly the right recipe to get over the lies and duplicity of Ryan once and for all, to put the "kisses like wine" promises behind her. But now was just not the time to be distracted. She had an unfortunate history of throwing away golden opportunities, and Paris was a temptation, *not* an opportunity.

Plus, she had seen a video of how airlines treated guitars. Her guitar was sulky enough at the moment.

Naturally, Sam would think she was crazy if she shared the fact that the needs of her temperamental guitar were part of what she needed to consider.

Was she crazy? Who thought their guitar talked to them? Or didn't, as the case might be.

"Have you heard the expression *no means no*?" Allie asked him.

"I've heard *of* it," he said. "Have I heard it personally? As in addressed to me? No. Of course not."

Of course not.

"I don't think you are using it in context," he told her. "I'm not propositioning you. The exact opposite, in fact."

"Oh!"

"It seems faintly inappropriate for you and I to consider staying under the same roof for any length of time, when we don't know each other. Red underwear notwithstanding."

"I told you it wasn't underwear," she protested, but knew he would be satisfied by the blush she could not control making her face feel hot.

"I'm not sure if you have a boyfriend," he continued persuasively, "or a mother, but I'm pretty sure neither of them would approve."

"I don't have a boyfriend, anymore," she snapped.

Sam tilted his head at her, pouncing on the one thing she did not want him to pounce on. "Anymore?"

She regretted adding that *anymore* instantly, as if her whole pathetic history was now on display. She wanted her lack of boyfriend to make her sound like an independent woman and not like a loser.

She diverted the talk—she hoped skillfully—away from the boyfriend. "Of course I have a mother. I'm quite used to her disapproval."

Used to it did not mean that she did not long for its opposite, had in fact spent most of her life longing for it, not that she would let that show on her face.

He looked surprised by that, as if she did not look like the kind of girl who earned her mother's disapproval. She felt a ridiculous desire to defend herself: *It's not my fault.* Instead, she stuck out her chin at him, and said, "I am not going anywhere."

"You need to think about that."

"No, I don't."

"Yes, you do."

She suddenly became aware of the stillness at the table and cast her gaze toward Cody. He had lost interest in his muffin, and his wide eyes were going from her to his uncle anxiously.

His uncle looked at Cody at the same time. He glared at her as if this was her fault, and then he smiled reassuringly at his nephew. "How's that muffin, big guy?"

Cody did not look the least reassured. Or like he thought the argument was her fault. He frowned at his uncle. At least one person seemed completely immune to Sam Walker's considerable charm.

Why did it make her feel a little sad that it was his nephew? If the child was, indeed, his nephew.

"Let's step outside for a moment," Sam suggested.

"Good idea." All the better to grill him about parental abduction!

"Why can't you leave?" he asked her in a low voice once they were on the deck.

"I have a deadline."

"For what?"

None of your business would be the appropriate answer, but she cast Cody another glance through the patio door, and knew she had to be civil for the child's sake. There was something very fragile about the boy. Plus, if she gave a little information, maybe Sam would be lulled into reciprocating with a little information of his own. "I write. Songs."

Not that her deadline was a song, exactly. In fact, once upon a time, she might have found her contract a bit humiliating. Apparently her guitar still disapproved, as if writing jingles for money was tawdry and superficial and would turn her into some kind of character from a sitcom.

But she had *finally* landed a contract for writing jingles. Paul's Steakhouse was due next week. It could lead to other things. It *would* lead to other things. Charlie Harper's success was nothing to sneeze at. If she delivered. If she showed she could be creative and commercial, plus disciplined enough to meet impossible deadlines.

"I knew it," he said. "Artsy. Paris would be perfect for songwriting."

"No, it would not," she said firmly. She would not allow herself to be distracted by Paris, and he would never understand about the guitar liking it here. "Every single thing I've ever written that was any good has been written here."

He looked like he got that, however reluctantly. "So, what do you suggest?"

"Couldn't you go to Paris?"

"No. There's nothing there for a three-year-old."

Here was her opportunity. "What is you and Cody's relationship?" she asked.

"I told you, he's my nephew."

"That's not what I meant."

"I'm his guardian." His voice was low. "My sister was his mom."

"Was?"

There was a long pause. For a moment the pain in Sam's eyes was so white hot, Allie felt as if she could be burned to ash by it.

"She died," he said, his voice low. "Her and her husband, in a car accident."

This was as unexpected as a slap. Allie felt her indignation dying in the light of this much larger revelation. She could barely speak for the emotion that clawed at her throat.

"That's why Cody doesn't talk," she whispered.

Something sagged in Sam's magnificent

shoulders, as if the weight of what he carried suddenly became too much for him to carry alone.

"His pediatrician says to give it time."

"How long has it been?"

"Eight months." He turned from her abruptly, looked out at the sea. "I don't know about this time thing. I don't know if it heals all wounds. My parents died in an accident, too, when I was just eighteen."

He looked as if he regretted saying that as soon as the words came out of his mouth. But she was left with an almost stunning awareness, not just that he was alone, but that he would have a terrible time trusting life. Worse than her.

In fact, her own wounds suddenly seemed to pale into insignificance. She missed Gram every day, but Mavis had known she was sick and her attitude and acceptance had helped Allie deal with the loss.

I'm old, she had said, patting Allie's hand. *This is the way of it—the old ones go, and the new ones come.*

But Sam's losses were completely different. They were unnatural and unexpected and he'd been blindsided by them. It felt as if Allie should know what to say—Gram would have known what to say—but she didn't and her silence coaxed more words from him.

"In some misguided moment," he continued, his voice a rasp of pure pain, "where Sue and Adam thought nothing bad could ever happen to them—despite the fact our family already had had terrible things happen—they named me as Cody's guardian in their will. They were probably having a glass of wine when they decided. I bet they laughed. I bet Sue said to Adam, 'Let's name Sam as guardian. That would be hilarious. He can't even keep a plant alive.'"

Allie moved beside him. Where words failed her, an instinct made her put her hand on his arm. In that place where there were no words, she needed to touch him.

He looked away from the water, and glared down at her hand, and she withdrew it rapidly, remembering her instincts were often so wrong.

"We're meeting some family here," Sam said, his voice gruff. "They've rented a place down the beach. They're coming from a great distance, and the arrangements have been in place for some time. That's why we can't go anywhere else."

There was something about the formality of all this, and the way he said *family*, with just a touch of hesitation, that told her what the answer to her next question was going to be. Still, she had to ask.

"And you can't move in with them?"

He shook his head, firmly, no.

"Well, then, we'll have to share."

"Share?"

Share—that concept five-year-olds learn in kindergarten. But somehow the sarcasm died within her before she spoke it.

"I'll stay out of your way," she promised. That was a vow she would keep, because looking at him she was suddenly aware there were distractions much bigger than Paris. "And you stay out of mine."

He looked annoyed. "This house is probably less than nine hundred square feet. Pretty hard to stay out of anyone's way."

"You could consider the beach an extension of the house."

"I don't want the family to get the wrong impression," he said, his voice a growl.

"The wrong impression?"

"Like you and I are cohabitating. Obviously, they would think that was bad for Cody."

Suddenly, she understood something far more than what he was saying was going on here. He did not look like the kind of man who gave two figs what anyone thought.

"What's the family connection of the people visiting?"

"It's my brother-in-law Adam's family. From Australia."

Something shivered along her spine. She could not take her eyes off his face. "Are they seeking custody of Cody?"

CHAPTER SEVEN

SAM DELIBERATELY LOOKED away from her. He did not like how astute she was, how she read him so easily, how she voiced a fear he had not even articulated inside himself.

He focused on the beach. There was a beach-comber out there this morning using a metal detector to look for treasure. One person's loss could be another person's gain. Beyond him, the waves lapped at the shore. He made him-self look at Allie.

She had obviously made a huge effort to cover up this morning. She looked like an "after" pic-ture for a weight-loss spa. She was dressed in too-large sweatpants and a shapeless T-shirt. It looked as if she could hold open the waistband of those pants and stick three more of her in there.

But no matter what Allie did, or what she wore, he could not un-see what he had seen last night. Or un-feel what he had felt when she was pressed against him on that bed.

Add that physical awareness of her—sharp in the air between them—to her kind of spooky intuition, and you had an equation that equaled trouble.

Still, had Sam actually ever put that question into words? Though the feeling of unease had gnawed at him, there was the question, point-blank. Did Adam's family, his brother, Bill, and his sister-in-law, Kathy, want custody?

"They haven't said those words," Sam admitted.

They hadn't said those words, and he hadn't said those words, but everyone would want what was best for Cody. And that was the million-dollar question, wasn't it? What was best for Cody? A single guy? Or a family?

One person's loss could be another person's gain.

He could feel her thoughtful eyes on him, scanning, picking up the things he was not saying. He felt as if she could see, or sense, the sinking in his stomach and the tightening in his heart.

"We'll make sure there are no wrong impressions," she promised.

We. As if they were a team.

"I'll stay out of your way," she promised again. "If they happen to meet me, we'll just have to explain the mix-up over the contract.

There will be no doubt in their minds that we are not involved in some casual fling. Besides, I think it would be pretty obvious to them, or anyone really, that a guy like you wouldn't be involved with someone like me."

Now she had his full attention. He could feel a frown pulling down his brows.

"Why would you say that?" he asked cautiously. That was certainly not what he had felt when he held her last night.

And not what he had felt at all when she had thrown her arms open to the spray of water from the garden hose, transforming her into a goddess of the night and sea.

He had felt the very real danger of some chemistry building between them.

"Oh, you know," she said breezily, "corporate king, beach-dwelling, barely-making-it musician."

"Corporate king?" he sputtered, vaguely insulted. "That's a weird conclusion to arrive at. It can't be the way I dress. You've seen me in shorts and sandals, and my pajamas, for Pete's sake."

"Ha. *GQ* on vacation. I bet you have a corner office, in a glass building with a stunning view. You probably built some kind of empire, from the ground up. Computer tech of some sort."

He could feel his brows knitting closer together, and made a conscious effort to relax them. "Did you do an internet search on me?"

"Aha! I'm right, then. I might have tried to do an internet search. Just to make sure there was no abduction afoot. Do you know how many Sam Walkers there are?"

"I have no idea."

"Thousands. No, it's the flashy car in the driveway, legal beagles ready to defend your contracts...everything about you radiates wealth and power. You send out the unmistakable tycoon vibe—"

"*Tycoon*? Me? I get a picture of a bunch of people stranded on a tropical island, and the tycoon being the snotty one who won't get his hands dirty."

"I was thinking something more current. Like the tech wizard, Mitch Jones. He's the guy who invented that app—"

"I know who he is," he said drily.

"Or that guy who created the company that morphed into the big search engine—"

"Henrich Pfitzer," he said.

"See? You know him. I knew it. Computer tech billionaires. They're your tribe."

"I don't know him! They are *not* my tribe. I don't have a tribe."

"Yes, you do."

He thought of telling her his "tribe" had

shrunk quite a bit in the past eight months. Popsy and Cody. He was barely at the office anymore, running things remotely, putting good, good people in charge. But she didn't know that, and what's more, she didn't need to know that.

"It's the *I have arrived* tribe," Allie told him, "whereas, I, on the other hand…"

She lifted a slender shoulder in wry self-deprecation that was somehow heart-wrenching.

Or would be if you had a heart, which he reminded himself, sternly, he no longer did.

"Anyway, it would be more than obvious to the casual observer, that you and I would be a terrible combination. Unworkable."

He should have found that conclusion a relief. Instead he found it somewhat distressing and found himself studying her. Sam became aware some hurt practically shimmered in the air around her.

Something—or more likely someone—had stolen her confidence from her.

He *hated* that. But he acknowledged he would be the worst possible choice to try to fix it. He had failed spectacularly at marriage. After the demise of his marriage, Sam had embraced a play-hard lifestyle. His sister had been fond of telling him that he had the emotional depth of a one-celled organism.

And all that was before more grief and a troubled nephew and a depressed dog had turned his life and his world upside down. It shocked him that he still projected the old him: wealthy and powerful, self-assured with the world at his feet. That's not what he was anymore.

He was a man who woke up every morning with a new sense of drowning in his own inadequacy.

You didn't grab onto someone else when you were drowning.

He knew that from a brief stint as a lifeguard when he was a teenager. A drowning person just pulled others down, too.

And two drowning people? Catastrophe.

"I don't see that we have a choice," she continued when he was silent. "We'll have to share the accommodation."

As if it was that simple: as if there was no history. No her coming at him with Harold, and no red bathing suit.

Last night, after the house had gone quiet, he had heard a door squeak open. And then another.

He'd gotten up and looked.

Popsy had always only been loyal to two people. Cody and Sam's sister.

Last night, the dog had managed to open the door of Cody's room and Sam had peered through the partially open door of Allie's to see the dog snuggled up with her on her bed.

Both door latches were worn out.

"You needn't worry," she assured him brightly, as if his worry at the brief but compelling history between them was written all over his face. "At all. Even if I was your type—so obvious I'm not—I'm not in the market for a relationship. Been there, done that."

She rolled her eyes as if her *been there, done that* meant nothing, but if he was not mistaken, that was a badly bruised heart she was wearing on her sleeve.

He shouldn't ask. But he did. "How old are you?"

"Why do you want to know?"

"Because you seem awfully young to have given up on happily-ever-after already."

"I'm twenty-three," she said, as if that was plenty old to have given up on romantic dreams.

"To be frank, you look like a poster child for picket fences and baby carriages, like those are the things that would make you happy."

"What a terribly old-fashioned thing to say." Bright spots rose up in her cheeks that told him he had hit a nerve.

"Ah, me and Thurston Howell are like that," he said. "Old-fashioned tycoon types."

"So, we both have some misperceptions we have to give up. How old are you?"

"Twenty-eight."

"And where are you at with *happily-ever-after*?"

He was annoyed by the question, but in fairness, he *had* started it.

"I gave it a try," he admitted, reluctantly. "I was married. I'm pretty good at math, so I should have realized, statistically, a fairy-tale ending was a long shot."

Why had he felt compelled to reveal that? For a frightening moment, he thought she was going to probe that, delve into his very private life. He could tell she was tempted. But, in the end, she didn't.

"My point exactly," Allie said. "I gave it a try, too. So, if we've dispensed with the personal part of the roommate arrangement, maybe we could move on?"

"To?"

"I can't seem to find the actual contract that you signed with my grandmother. Do you have a copy of it?"

"Not with me. It will be at my office. I can have someone send it, if you want. Is there something in particular you need clarified?"

"I was wondering if you already paid my

grandmother or if I can look forward to some funds?"

He suspected this was still about the relationship she was not planning on having with him. She wanted him to be aware of all the chasms that separated them, finances probably being the biggest one.

And she wanted it to look as if all she really cared about was the money, as if that was why she was agreeing to sharing her cottage with him. She wanted it to look as if she was capable of keeping this relationship strictly business.

"So Paris is completely off the table?"

"Completely," she said firmly. "I can't go anywhere else. Not right now."

He saw it. For one second, he saw something flash through those clear eyes. For all her brave front and businesslike tone, it was apparent Allie was terrified of going out into the larger world.

"My grandmother used to say the cure for anything is salt water," she said, though he was not sure which of them she thought needed curing, her or him.

"Salt water?" he asked, softly.

She looked at him. "It's a quote, she found in an old *Reader's Digest* from the thirties. Along with her fabric collection, my grandmother's closets are stuffed with those. The quote is,

'The cure for anything is salt water—sweat, tears or the sea.'"

It confirmed what he had glimpsed: something in her was afraid, hurt, broken. Seeking a cure, even in the brittle yellowed pages of old magazines. He should have known how deep the fear was in her when she tried to clobber him with Harold!

He didn't know the why of it—why such a beautiful young woman was hiding out here. He didn't actually *want* to know the why of it. He was shocked to find out there were enough pieces of his heart left intact to break some more. For her. Someone who was practically a stranger to him.

Suddenly, he saw the truth of it: if he insisted on her moving out, if he followed the letter of the law and enforced his contract, she was not going to see how sensible it was, how it would protect them both.

She was going to see it as more proof that the world was out of her control, that bad things could happen to her without warning, that this place where she felt safe was not safe, either.

He was not the man to fix whatever had gone wrong for her. He knew that. But he knew, as a person who had found out exactly that hard truth about the world—that there was no safe place— he could not make it any worse for her, either.

Sam took a deep breath and looked out over her shoulder again, at the perfect stretch of beach. The beachcomber had paused and was digging through the sand. He held something up to the sun, and it glittered gold.

Sam had been holding on to this place, in his mind, thinking long, summery days of sand and water could help Cody. Help *them* create the bond he felt was absent. Help them become a family, of sorts, or let go of that notion altogether. He had counted on this place, so special in his world, to help him know what to do.

The complication to his plan, Allie, turned and looked at the stretches of golden sand and gently lapping waves, too.

If she was prepared to keep it all business, so was he. That was his specialty, after all, business. It was apparent she needed the money.

But it was her words, not her need of money, that he was thinking of. *Sweat, tears or the sea.*

Her words held a promise of something. Hope.

Which, of course, was the most dangerous thing of all.

So, maybe not the wisest thing to share a space with her but, as she had pointed out, they could avoid each other.

They could use the beach as an extension of the house. Though Sam did not consider himself intuitive—at all—he had a deep sense of Cody *needing* the beach, that carefree place of sandcastles and kites and leaping waves.

Besides, he didn't have any choice, really.

Life had been showing him that lately. He didn't always have choices. He hated that. He hated feeling powerless, as if the most important things in life could be wrested from his control in an instant.

"Okay," he heard himself saying. "I thought these days were well behind me, but let's be roommates."

She held out her hand to shake on it.

He hesitated, and then took it. The full danger of what he was letting himself in for was in the delicate strength and vulnerability of her touch.

And yet, somehow in that touch, too, was a sense of having, impossibly, found something gold in a vast expanse of sand.

He sighed. One more complication in a life that was already way too complicated.

CHAPTER EIGHT

THERE, ALLIE THOUGHT, it was official. They were roommates.

She felt something when they shook hands. A jolt. A tingle. She couldn't deny that. But she had spoken the absolute truth to him: she was done with chasing happily-ever-after. She hated it that he saw picket fences and baby carriages in her, as if wisps of her unrealistic dreams clung to her like a mist.

But he was done with dreams, too. He'd been married. And it hadn't worked. For some reason that surprised her, maybe because of what she'd seen in his interactions with Cody in just this short time.

He didn't look like a man who gave up on love. He didn't look like a man who would take a vow and then break it.

But whatever, life had made him cynical and her cynical and what could be more perfect for both of them?

Except there was something about Sam Walker's desperate I'll-never-give-up-on-you love for his nephew that had just cracked open some barrier around her heart that she would have sworn was made of stone.

And that jolt she had felt when their hands touched? That was a power she might be very foolish to feel she could control. So, yes, the best plan was avoidance.

Easy for two weeks.

Strictly business.

"So do you owe me anything?" she asked, crisply.

He told her how much he owed her and her mouth fell open. It was everything she could do to prevent herself from dancing a little jig. She didn't care how much she had to suffer for the next two weeks. It was worth it.

Three full days later, Allie realized she might have been a little overconfident in assessing her own ability to suffer the inconveniences of having two roommates thrust into her world, one totally adorable, and the other totally sexy.

Oh, they had managed to work out the small details of living together. Sam was startled that the television was gone, but adjusted quickly, and played morning cartoons for Cody on his tablet. They provided their own groceries and the top two shelves of the fridge were his, the bathroom was set aside at seven each night for Cody's bath, she surrendered the porch and went for a walk and swim every afternoon so that Sam could have it to read during Cody's nap time.

But still, sharing quarters with an absolutely gorgeous man, a sweet small child and a dog who could melt the heart of Attila the Hun, all the while maintaining a suitably aloof distance, was difficult.

The house took on their presence.

When Sam noticed things that needed repair, he just did it, casually, without fanfare, and with a certain enviable male confidence, as if wielding a hammer and a screwdriver so naturally was just what real men did, as if it was nothing to get things ship-shape.

The evidence of the men in her life was suddenly everywhere: a shirt left on the swing, large flip-flops beside small ones at the back door, a small truck on the table, a partially completed Lego structure on the back deck, a load of underwear left in the dryer.

A radio was left on. She had long since stopped listening to the radio, but thankfully it was on a classical station, no gossipy chit-chat. A book, a memoir of surviving the Second World War, not a suspense thriller, was left open on its spine on the table on the back deck. She told herself she hated people who left books open on their spines, even while she looked at his reading material with way more interest than she should. She overheard him having conversations with his office that underscored that he was as confident and powerful in that world as he was adorably inept in his "daddy" role.

She felt like a detective collecting clues to who he was.

And who Sam was, was in his voice as he read stories to Cody. It was in the kitchen, where she saw that his culinary skills were clumsy, and ran to peanut butter on crackers, frozen fish sticks and fries, order-in pizzas.

It was watching from the porch as the two of them, Sam and Cody, headed across the beach, in the morning. Cody's little chest and face glistening white with generously applied sunscreen, his shoulders covered by his Superman cape. As far as she could tell, Sam wore no sunscreen at all.

It was feeling her heart squeeze at the sight of the small hand in a large one, towels tucked under Sam's arm, sand toys and buckets held firmly in his free hand. It was feeling something sigh within her when they returned, sleeping pale boy over Sam's broad, sun-kissed shoulder, as he juggled all their other items, the sand-encrusted Superman cape tied around his own shoulders.

But Sam Walker, not just as a daddy, but as a man, also emerged. The scent of him. The encounters. His hand accidentally brushing hers as they both reached into the fridge. The shared laughter when Popsy licked a spill off the floor.

She had practically smacked into him this morning when he had come out of the shower dressed only in a towel.

It had done things to her pulse that were not in the Roommates Rules of Order.

Now, within hours, she had nearly smacked into him again in the same hallway. This time he was wearing only shorts. "Thought you were out," he said, by way of apology.

She had been out.

"I thought you were out," she said. She had come back in that red bikini they had a shared history with.

"Cody needed the bathroom."

There they were, nearly naked together again. It seemed criminal that he was so perfectly made, his skin turning golden from the beach days. She wanted to touch it.

Some unmistakable heat sizzled in the air between them.

"Thanks for fixing things," she said, trying

to find safe ground. "The front door bell, the kitchen faucet, the cupboard doors."

"It's nothing. I used to do it for Mavis, too."

"I noticed you fixed the latch on my bedroom door."

"I didn't think you'd appreciate the nocturnal visits from Popsy."

"I actually kind of like them," she admitted. Then blushed, as if she had said she didn't like sleeping alone. "Now that I know it's not a burglar, that is."

"I noticed you haven't been locking the patio doors at night."

"Should I?" She had felt totally safe since that night they had stood outside together rinsing off the dog.

He smiled. "I sleep pretty light. I'll look after you."

That was what had been creeping into her house without her being aware of it. A sense of being looked after. Protected. She could see how ferocious he would be if she and Cody needed protecting.

It made something warm unfurl in her stomach.

She could argue she didn't need his protection. Or his fixes. But she didn't feel like arguing about it.

In fact, she felt deeply and dangerously aware

of what he had brought to her house. She lifted her hand. Was she going to touch him? Why?

Just some gratitude bubbling within her that needed to find expression...the bathroom door burst open and Cody raced out.

Sam stood, frozen.

Just for a second, until they heard small footsteps pounding across the back deck. It broke the spell between them.

"Hey," Sam yelled, racing after him. "Did you wash your hands?"

The cottage was suddenly too quiet, and Allie stood there, feeling as if they had had a near miss of some sort. Had she been about to touch him?

She brushed her fringe out of her eyes, as if she could convince herself *that* had been her intention all along.

It felt more imperative than ever to put distance between them, but Cody went for his nap early that day, and their paths crossed again as Sam settled on the deck.

"See you later," she said breezily, coming out the back door, a very proper swim cover-up in place.

"Yeah, have a good afternoon."

Something in his voice stopped her. She noticed he wasn't reading his book, but gazing out at the beach. The afternoon crowds had begun to arrive. The scent of coconut oil drifted up to her, and bright umbrellas dotted the sand. An inflated ball blew out to sea as a little girl shrieked her outrage at its loss.

There was something in the quietness around him that made her stop partway down the stairs and come back up them.

"Sam?"

He pulled his attention away from the beach.

"Are you okay?" she asked.

"Sure. Yeah."

Something made her wait instead of taking his words at face value.

"It's just that they're arriving tomorrow. My in-laws. I guess they're my in-laws. What do you call the relatives of your in-laws? Are they in-laws, too?"

She was seeing what she suspected was a very rare flagging in his confidence. Her need to preserve her own sanity fled. She pulled out a chair at the table.

"Cody's aunt and uncle and cousins are arriving tomorrow," he clarified.

"What are their names?" she asked him softly.

"Bill. That's my brother-in-law, Adam's brother. His wife is Kathy. Their kids are Nicole and Bryan."

"Then that's what you call them."

He nodded. "Of course. Simple." But his voice sounded strained. "It's not as if they're strangers. I've met them. Half a dozen times. We video chat. *I* video chat. Try to think of things to say, because Cody can't."

"They'll see how good you are with Cody," she assured him. "I have."

Sheesh! She might as well admit she had been spying on him.

But he didn't seem to notice. "Will they? Don't you think they'll look at him not talking, after all this time, and wonder what the hell I'm doing? I haven't actually told them he doesn't talk. Maybe I should have sent a memo, I don't know."

"They must have figured it out from the video chats," she told him gently.

"His cousin, Nicole, is six. She fills all the silences. She sings to him, sometimes she'll read a story. But surely they've noticed he doesn't speak, surely they've wondered about it every time we've done the video thing. Maybe that's why they're coming."

"I think they'll look at you and see a man doing the best that he can."

His voice was very low. "I'm afraid it's not good enough. That's my fear. That my best is not good enough. For Cody. And that that will be immediately obvious to anyone looking."

She felt his pain and his desperation. "It's not obvious to me," she said softly.

She did what she had wanted to do since she had found herself cuddled up to him that first night. She touched him. Only not in the same way she had wanted to touch him then.

She reached across the space that separated them, and touched his cheek. She could feel the rough, sensuous scrape of his whiskers beneath her fingertips, beneath that, the sharp and glorious contrast that was the silk of his skin.

But more than the physical sensation of touching him, Allie felt what he was feeling. His tremendous insecurity. His desire to do the right thing by his nephew, even at personal cost to himself.

She could feel the depth and strength of his love, and she was tremendously moved by it.

"It's going to be okay," she said.

His eyes met hers, and she could see he longed to believe her. He looked like a drowning man who had been thrown a life preserver.

He covered her hand with his own. It seemed like the most natural thing in the world when he slid her hand toward his mouth, and kissed it.

"Thank you," he said, his voice a soft growl of pure emotion. "Thank you, Allie."

She looked at where her hand rested against his lips. She *felt* the exquisiteness of his lips touching her skin. She felt it as intensely as she had ever felt anything: as if the crowds on the beach and the slap of the waves, the dog at their feet, Cody snoozing away in his bedroom, all faded.

This became her whole world.

His lips.

Her skin.

Part of her was amazed that her hand was not smoking, pre-ignition. The awareness of him that had been building in her for days felt as if it exploded.

She grabbed her hand away from him.

Suddenly protecting herself felt imperative again. Sam as *vulnerable* and strong and loving was just too potent a combination. It made her heart hurt.

"Well," she said, standing up, straightening her swim cover, "off I go."

She tried to act casual as she went off the porch and walked through the sand, dodging umbrellas and people to find herself at the water's edge. She tried to act as if her whole world had not just shifted on its axis.

Allie shucked her swim cover, and hurled herself into the waves, certain that she could hear a sizzle as her overheated self hit the cold water.

And she was sure she could feel his gaze as it followed her. And it was overheated, too.

CHAPTER NINE

BEYOND THE UMBRELLAS and the people, Sam could still see Allie. He watched as she arrived at the ocean's edge and dropped her swim cover.

She was wearing a one-piece bathing suit today, turquoise and navy shades swirling together. The back was an open U, dipping just below her hipbones, leaving the tenderness of her neck exposed, and her naked back. Her skin was golden and flawless. The bathing suit was every bit as sexy as the bikini had been. He felt mesmerized by her, and was relieved when she flung herself into the ocean with a kind of reckless abandon.

He contemplated the gift she had just given him. He didn't know which was more dangerous: the physical allure of her or the emotional sanctuary.

She believed in him.

He hadn't known he had needed that. He was

a man who had always believed in himself. He did not know why it meant so much to him.

She barely knew him, or Cody, for that matter. And yet, they shared a space. She probably, at this point, knew more about his and Cody's relationship than any other living being, aside from Popsy, who hardly counted.

Popsy, who crept out of Cody's room every night, pushed open Allie's door and climbed into her bed. Now that Sam had fixed the latch, Allie must be letting the dog in, because Sam still woke in the morning to Popsy slinking out of Allie's room, as if he had been caught in an indiscretion.

The indiscretion being that Popsy had never once slept with Sam.

"And that is going to be the only indiscretion in this house," Sam muttered, as he watched Allie swim out past the wave break, and begin a strong crawl across the mouth of the bay. He decided, when Cody woke up, they would go out for dinner.

A good strategy, because when they came back, the house was empty. It was only after Cody's bath that Sam realized he had forgotten to get milk while they were out.

Cody was already in his pajamas, but sometimes he was upset by small changes to his routines. With that one notable exception, when he'd had the muffin Allie brought him for breakfast, he ate cereal for breakfast. Bits O' Goodness, nothing else.

The counselor had told Sam that Cody's rigidity about his routines, and what he ate, were a way of trying to make his world safe and predictable.

Since tomorrow they were meeting his aunt and uncle and his cousins, it didn't seem like it would be a good morning to test the waters with a new breakfast, say of toast, or waffles.

Sam wanted the day to be perfect, not to start with friction between him and Cody, or with one of Cody's meltdowns.

There had been no meltdowns, he realized, since they'd arrived. The long days of sunshine, water, sand, were doing everything he hoped.

"Come on, buddy, let's get dressed and go get some milk."

Cody shook his head, vehemently, *no*.

Which would be safer? A small disruption to the bedtime routine now, or trying out something new for breakfast tomorrow?

"You can pick some things. It will be fun. You like the grocery store. You can pick cookies."

Cody shook his head, no, again, then dashed by his uncle at lightning speed. He went out the back door and, thankfully, skidded to a halt when he saw Allie out there, her guitar across her lap, a blank piece of paper beside her and a pencil behind her ear.

Sam came out. She'd been so quiet he hadn't realized she was home. He certainly hadn't heard a guitar.

"Come on," he wheedled. "Chocolate chip."

"What's up?" Allie said.

"Uh, we're out of milk. I thought I'd make a quick run to the store. I'm bribing Cody to come with me. Please don't tell me bribing is not part of good parenting."

She smiled at him. "I'm no expert on good parenting. You can go for milk if you want, me and Cody can hang for a bit."

"I don't remember that being part of our arrangement."

"Well, sometimes life requires flexibility." She ran her thumb over the strings of her guitar. The notes were rich and full. Definitely a sound Sam would have noticed if it had happened before.

She didn't even look at Cody, but ran her thumb over the strings again. "You want to hang with me while your uncle goes and gets groceries?"

Sam could feel himself holding his breath. Cody didn't like letting his uncle out of his sight.

But Cody looked at her, then nodded with a certain insulting vehemence.

"Sheesh," Sam said.

"Before I got sidetracked, I took two years of early childhood education at university, so I'm imminently qualified for half an hour of child care." Allie strummed at her guitar, took the pencil from behind her ear, wrote something down, frowned and crossed it out.

"My guitar hates Paul's Steakhouse," she muttered.

"I ate there once. I hated it, too."

She groaned. "Don't tell me that. I'm supposed to be writing a jingle for their radio ad."

"Like a character on a sitcom?"

She shot him an annoyed look. "Kind of like that," she said. "Only without the sleazy part. Or the fabulously wealthy part."

Cody settled on the floor of the porch in front of her. He raised his arms in the air and made fluttering movements with his fingers.

Allie glanced up from her guitar, shot Sam a puzzled look. He frowned.

"I think maybe he's requesting a song," Allie said.

Sam looked from her to his nephew, and then recognized exactly what Cody was doing. "You're right! His Aussie cousin Nicole sings him that one. On the video conferences. 'Inky-dinky Spider.'"

"Oh!" Excited, Allie began strumming her guitar. "It's 'itsy-bitsy,' not 'inky-dinky.'"

"Thank you," he said drily. "I consider myself edified."

She ignored him, strummed the guitar, fiddled with the frets and then began to sing.

"The itsy-bitsy spider," she sang, playing simple, accompanying notes on the guitar, *"went up the water spout."*

Sam felt a quiver go up and down his spine. The guitar made a sound he had never heard an instrument make before: as if it had its own voice.

"Down came the rain and washed the spider out."

And Allie's voice was beyond incredible. Nothing in the way she spoke could have prepared him for the tone of it, rich, deep, sensuous.

"Out came the sun and dried up all the rain."

It seemed suddenly as if the world was infused with that very sun she was singing about, as if light had come out from behind a rain cloud and made the world sparkling and new. Cody was sweeping his arms from side to side, forming a semi-circle for the sun. For a suspended moment, Sam was aware of the corn silk color of Cody's hair, the roundness of his cheeks, the thickness of his lashes.

The light extended to Allie. Sam felt as if he was nearly vibrating with awareness of her, of the unconscious sensuality of her fingers as she strummed, of the light playing with the black tips of her sun-streaked hair, of the golden tone of her skin and of the plumpness of her lower lip. He was aware of the way her too-large light blue button-up shirt had slid off the slenderness of her shoulder, revealing a bra strap as white as snow. He was aware of the snugness of her shorts, and sun-browned legs, and bare toes tapping the rough wood of the porch.

"And the itsy-bitsy spider climbed up the spout again."

Her voice was rich, it was stunning, it was magical, the kind of voice that could weave a web of enchantment around the unwary, that could wake a man who had been sleeping, that could make him so acutely aware of everything around him, and of his own heartbeat and the summer heat coming off his skin, that it felt almost painful to be alive, to be breathing.

Was that silly song really about life? Climbing up, being washed down, the sun coming out and giving you the courage to try again?

The enchantment seemed to have oozed over

Cody like warmed honey. He clapped with delight. He smiled! Not that secretive little smile that sometimes Sam caught sight of, as Cody moved into his imaginary world of superheroes and cars, but an open, engaged smile of pure delight.

"You're really good at this," she encouraged Cody. He puffed up under her approval. She began the song again at the beginning.

Cody swayed happily, and acted out the sequence.

First the dog, and now Cody, Sam thought, watching, trying to hide the fact that this small event was making him feel alive, his nephew's obvious pleasure was making him extraordinarily emotional.

"What?" Allie asked, glancing at him.

"Nothing," Sam mumbled. But it wasn't nothing.

He thought of asking her if she was an enchantress. That's how he felt, with her music, her beautiful voice washing over him, as if he could follow the dog and his nephew and fall, fall, fall under her spell.

The worst possible thing he could do was give himself over to it. She'd agreed to hold down the fort. He needed to go get milk. But instead, in the grip of something larger than him, and larger than all of them, Sam found himself sinking onto the deck, cross-legged, beside Cody.

"Can you do 'Do Your Ears Hang Low?'" Sam asked her.

"Of course."

Allie sang every rollicking, motion-based children's song that she knew. And then she slowed it down and sang quieter songs, until finally she was singing lullabies.

At some point, Cody climbed onto Sam's lap, inserted his thumb in his mouth, and despite his fighting it, his eyes finally closed and stayed that way. His warmth puddled against Sam and made him feel the glorious and terrifying pull of pure love.

Sam got up, his nephew in his arms, and went into the house. He tucked Cody in and stared down at the sleeping child, so aware of the gravity of his responsibility, so aware love complicated decisions—it didn't make them easier.

He untied the cape string, and tiptoed out and shut the door. He told himself not to go back out on that deck, but how could he not thank her for the look he had seen on Cody's face?

"He didn't even wake up for bedtime stories," he said. "It's the second time today I feel like I owe you a big thank-you."

"Not at all. That was really fun for me, too."

He came and sank down on the swing beside her. It felt as if it was the most natural thing in the world.

"I saw something tonight that I wasn't sure I'd ever see again," Sam confided in her. "While you were singing, Cody was the way he used to be. I mean, not talking. But happy. Especially with his aunt and uncle coming tomorrow, that means so much to me."

His hand found hers, again as if it was the most natural thing in the world. He squeezed it. Some part of him wanted to hang on. Forever.

Despite the itsy-bitsy spider encouraging him to try again and again, Sam knew the saddest lesson of all. There was no forever.

He slid his hand from the warmth of hers.

Allie loved the weight of Sam on the swing beside her, the gentle creak as he shoved it back and forth with the balls of his feet.

"It made me happy, too," she admitted, "in a way I haven't been for a long time."

He stopped pushing the swing back and forth with his feet. He looked at her, ran his hand through his hair, looked toward the darkened beach, the moonlight capping the waves in snow-white froth. He was making a decision, Allie thought, whether to go or whether to stay here with her.

"Allie, how come you haven't been happy?" His voice was a rasp.

She was aware they were standing at a crossroads, of sorts. Life had taught her it was dangerous to trust people. Just like Sam, she had a decision to make right now, too.

So did she protect herself? Or did she throw caution to the wind?

CHAPTER TEN

WAS ALLIE READY to open up, to anyone, let alone Sam Walker? She could feel herself lean-ing away from what he was offering.

But then it was as if she heard her grand-mother's voice. *A burden is made lighter for sharing it.* She knew she would feel lighter if the secret she carried was revealed.

"Tell me about how your life got side-tracked," he invited softly. "It seems to me you would have made the best teacher ever."

She contemplated that, that he had listened to her. Why not tell him what had happened to her? The stars were winking out, he was a solid presence beside her, she had seen his gentle, firm way with Cody.

Why not trust him?

Because the world has taught you the dan-ger of trusting, a voice inside her said, and this time it was not her grandmother's voice.

To her surprise, she chose to ignore that voice. She chose to throw caution to the wind.

"I had just completed my sophomore year at university. It was a small campus, so everyone was shocked, and really excited, that the show *American Singing Star* chose us as a location to hold tryouts. People knew I sang, and everyone wanted me to try out. There was quite a lucrative financial prize, so there I found myself in front of a panel of judges."

"*American Singing Star*? The television show?" he asked.

She had the horrifying thought he might have seen her spectacular fall from grace. "Yes, have you seen it?"

"No, I have to say television isn't my thing. Until Cody. Now it's *SpongeBob SquarePants*, *Rugrats*, *Doug*. But I know what it is. Kind of an offshoot of that really famous reality singing show, right?"

"Yes, that's the one. Anyway, I did fairly well. I got to the finals. And then I failed. It was quite a ride, from soaring successes to utter humiliation, all conducted under the unforgiving lens of the public eye."

"That seems like the short version," Sam said. "Why didn't you go back to school after it didn't pan out?"

"The whole thing was so public. For a while

everyone knew who I was." *And hated me.* "It's dying down now, a bit."

"So, you *are* hiding here," he said softly.

She shot him a look. "A conclusion you had already arrived at?"

He lifted a shoulder and looked at her, his eyes on her face making her feel there was no keeping secrets from him. "You're a lovely young woman who told me you don't believe in happily-ever-after. Why don't you tell me about that part?"

"Maybe another time," she said, thinking it would be way too easy to tell him everything.

"I can go look online," he said. "You already told me whatever happened played out publicly."

She sighed. The stars were winking on above them, and the waves were picking up. She could hear their gentle lapping turning into crashing. What would Gram tell her to do?

The temptation of being relieved in some way of this burden was too much to resist. To have someone, anyone, know the truth.

"At first," she said, "everything about that show was exciting. They gave me a different name, one of those one-name things like Cher. They redid the original audition tape, with me coming out and introducing myself as Tempest.

"Of course it was obvious I was the furthest thing from a tempest you could imagine. I was a small-town college kid in pigtails and jeans. One of the judges—the same one who suggested the change to one name—rolled his eyes. I should have realized how scripted everything was, right then, that it was really live theater. And maybe I did, but it was all so exciting.

"I kept getting put forward to the next round. I was like this instant celebrity—singers I'd admired were inviting me to their homes. There was talk of record deals and guest spots at concerts and collaborations. It was all very heady stuff."

"But?" he asked.

"They were telling me how to dress, and doing my hair and doing my makeup. They gave us a place to live—all the finalists in this fancy-fancy mansion built into the hills, with a pool. At the time it felt right. It felt as if this glossy, beautiful, beloved-by-the-public creature, *Tempest*, was who I was always meant to be.

"There was a guy in the same competition. We were under the same strains. Ryan was cute. He was friendly. I started leaning on him, and he on me. It became more and more romantic. I didn't realize how much of our relationship was being orchestrated. Looking back, there was probably a subplot in play from the first audition.

"The script probably read something like this—wholesome, small-town geek, whose music style is folksy, will fall for big-city super-suave rock star type. As the competition moves along, the geek will become more and more glamourous and superficial, and he will become more and more down-to-earth, with his heart on his sleeve.

"A romance among the two most popular contestants was great for the show. Imagine what that did for ratings! But I was oblivious to all that. Ryan was part of this exciting new future that was going to be mine. I was head over heels for him and I thought he was for me. He was always doing these crazy little things—presenting me with bouquets of dandelions, drawing hearts in lipstick on my dressing room mirror, sneaking kisses, making promises and plans.

"Gone was the studious girl whose greatest ambition had been to teach kindergarten, meet a nice guy someday, get married, have a few kids. Ryan insisted we were going to be as famous as other megastar couples and that our music and our love was our ticket to the whole world.

"The night before the final competition,

Ryan told me it was all fake. He'd been put up to the whole thing by the show's producers. He didn't love me. He didn't even think of the dandelion bouquets or the lipstick hearts himself.

"I was devastated. Did they know how devastated I would be? I don't know, but I think they did. I think I was played like a fiddle. I couldn't pull myself together for the final show. I didn't even want to win anymore. I didn't care enough.

"But he did. Oh, Ryan went on that final show, live, and talked about how I had broken him in two. He sang a heart-wrenching ballad about treachery and lost love. He even squeezed out a tear with his final note."

Sam said a word under his breath that he could not say around Cody, but that summed up how she felt *exactly*.

"This adoring public, this mega fan base, turned on me in a blink. I went from being America's sweetheart to the most hated person on the planet. I couldn't turn on a television set without some entertainment guru weighing in on it.

"Social media lit up with everyone commenting on how despicable I was. I cut my hair, and people still recognized me, though most weren't quite as nasty in person, thank goodness, as when they were hiding behind their keyboards.

Still, I had to wear a disguise to go get groceries, oversize sunglasses and a ball cap. Going back to school, where everyone had been so proud of me, seemed out of the question.

"And so I retreated to here. To my grandmother, who never lost sight of who I really was, even when I did, and to this place. She got rid of the television. She was sick, but she seemed to rally to help me. We played cards, and cooked and sewed together, and talked and talked and talked. Looking back it was the worst of times, because she was sick and I was hurting, but also the best of times, because we were together in such an intense, loving way.

"But I can't seem to write songs anymore, not even the jingle I've been hired to write. Tonight is the first time, in a long time, I've actually played my guitar and sang. And you know what was great about it? It wasn't about me. It was about the music bringing joy. Somehow, that's part of what I've lost."

She didn't realize she had started crying until he placed a finger on her cheeks and caught a tear.

And then he gathered her in his arms, and held her with such exquisite tenderness that she thought it was possible to die from it.

"My turn to thank you," she managed to choke out.

"That's a lot to carry by yourself," he said. "Where's your family in all this? Especially since Mavis died?"

"Humph," she said, against his chest.

"I remember you saying once, in passing, your mother disapproved of you. Because of this?"

She was stunned by how carefully he had listened and by how intuitive he was. Somehow, that was not what she would have expected from him.

"When people think of mothers they think of PTA and cookies, but my mom wasn't like that. She was a single mom, and darned proud of it, a career woman who made her own way. She referred to my father as *the donor*. I actually thought I was a product of a sperm bank.

"She was a professor of economics at that same small-town college I ended up going to. She was a nontraditional person in a very traditional town. I craved every single thing she eschewed about that town—neat little houses behind trimmed hedges, churches with Sunday services, marriage, families with mommies and daddies, babies. I wanted to celebrate normal Christmases, she wanted to shop and go to plays in New York. I wanted to spend summers here at the beach with my grandmother, but I only got a few weeks. The rest of the time I was dragged off to Europe with her.

"When I went to college to study early child-hood education, my mother was appalled. She saw that choice as reflecting a shocking lack of ambition. She wasn't totally behind the whole *American Singing Star* thing, but she applauded the ambition. She actually let it slip that maybe I took after my father. I wheedled it out of her that he'd been a college music teacher by day, and a guitar player in a band at night.

"She disliked Ryan, and saw our great ro-mance for what it was—a sham. She saw right through him. But if I expected sympathy after the big public humiliation, what I got instead was a kind of self-satisfied *I told you so*, as if being right was far more important to her than my feelings."

Sam said that word he couldn't say around Cody again. His fury on her behalf made her sniffle again.

"Anyway, she took a position as a visiting fellow at Oxford shortly after it all happened, and I came here."

"Aw, Allie…"

It was the genuine tenderness in his voice that undid her. The tears came, hard, soaking his chest.

"I'm sorry," she said. "This is the second time I've fallen apart on you, and gotten your shirt all wet. You'll think I'm such a crybaby. And nothing could be further from the truth."

"Liar," he said, and that same tender note in his voice kept it from stinging. At all.

Still, she felt honor bound to correct him. "No, really. It's not a lie. I'm very strong. Independent. Resilient."

"Uh-huh."

It was pretty hard to make a case for strength, when she'd already admitted she was hiding from the world. Suddenly, it did not feel like such a bad thing to be *seen*.

Allie just wanted to know what he saw. She pulled back from him, and studied his face. When had it become so familiar to her that she felt she knew every plane of it, and every nuance of expression?

"What do you see?" she asked, wondering if she was ready for his answer.

Without even a moment's hesitation, Sam said, "I see you as compassionate, sensitive, creative."

He lifted her chin with his finger and scanned her face. Her arguments caught in her throat.

"But not strong," she said.

"The world has quite enough strong people. The world needs you."

"Ha," she said.

"No, I'm not kidding. It's people like you,"

he told her softly, "who have the hardest job. You have to try and make the world more beautiful. Paint the pictures. Tell the stories. Sing the songs."

"I don't sing anymore. Not publicly, anyway."

He seemed to consider that, and then, as if words could not be enough to express what he was feeling, Sam lowered his head and touched his lips to her lips.

Not in a sexual way.

In a far more powerful way. In a way that said he saw her. And approved of what he saw.

But the kiss was like a tiny spark held to the dry tinder of her soul. Allie felt something white-hot blaze through her. She might have deepened that kiss into something quite different, but Sam stood up abruptly.

"Shoot. I forgot the milk," he said, his voice pure gravel, as he stared down at her. "I better go grab it before the store closes."

Sam drove away from the cottage feeling two things: a kind of helpless tenderness toward Allie, and a kind of impotent fury at the world and how it had treated her.

And maybe he reserved a touch of that impotent fury for himself. What was he thinking kissing his landlady?

But this went deeper, and he was aware he

had felt such fury only once before, when Sue and Adam had been killed.

The events, he knew, were not on the same scale, but the feeling was so similar: a kind of helplessness in the face of life's unfairness, in the face of cruelty to people who did not deserve it. Allie had been manipulated and betrayed and it made him so angry he wanted to punch someone.

Still, no matter what he was feeling, surely kissing her had not been a proper response to that?

And yet, what other way, to let her know, *he saw her.* In the past few days, he felt as if he had seen who she really was.

He knew he shouldn't do it, but he did it anyway. He pulled over to the side of the road and yanked out his phone.

He searched Tempest, *American Singing Star.* He only watched half of one of her performances.

It was not that she wasn't talented. It was not that she couldn't sing.

It was that he could barely recognize her with the long, jet-black hair, the false eyelashes, the form-fitting black leather outfit.

Watching her performance only intensified the helpless rage he felt at all of them: the show, Ryan, her mother.

He turned off the phone. He put the car back in Drive. He went to the store and got milk. It was on his way out the door of the store that he stopped, stunned by his realization.

For the first time since the accident had taken Adam and Sue, he genuinely cared about someone outside of the walls of his little world.

He wasn't ready.

And life hadn't asked him if he was.

CHAPTER ELEVEN

ALLIE MADE A point of not being up when Sam got back from the store. He'd made it clear he wished that brush of lips between them had not happened.

And it was humiliating that she felt the opposite. As if she would like it to happen and happen some more.

Embarrassing! In the morning, anxious to avoid more embarrassment, and the longing being in the same room as his lips was going to cause her, she was up and out the door before Sam and Cody were even out of bed. She took her guitar and some peanut butter sandwiches, and headed away from the beach—way too crowded in light of tomorrow's Fourth of July celebrations—and toward the hills that overlooked Sugar Cone.

It wasn't that she hadn't liked what Sam said to her but that she had liked it way, way too much. She needed to start crossing days off her calendar, a countdown to how many days before Sam and Cody would be gone.

Her life would be back to the way it was before.

Yawningly empty, a little voice informed her. And worse, all about her.

She found a favorite overlook with a bench and set up. By late afternoon, she had eaten her sandwiches, watched butterflies, listened to birds, talked with six strangers, petted several dogs and done a few yoga stretches.

What she hadn't done was made any progress on her jingle. Last night, she'd thought the creative block was over. Her guitar had been speaking to her again, humming like a living thing under her flying fingers as she sang to Cody and Sam.

Today the instrument was stubbornly and silently back on mute. The lyric part of the exercise was no better. Every time she thought of Paul's Steakhouse, the only thing she could think of that even remotely rhymed was *make-out.*

Which led her right back to the feel of Sam's lips on hers.

She couldn't concentrate. It had nothing to do with the taste of his lips. Or those words, those tender, beautiful words: *The world needs you.*

Oh, who was she kidding? It had everything to do with that kiss, and especially those words.

It felt to Allie as if those words were in some way pivotal. They were the words she had needed to hear her entire life. That there was not just a place in the world for her, but that it needed her.

And how was she repaying the kindness of those powerful words? Hiding. Just as he had accused her of doing.

Hiding from the world.

Hadn't she been hiding, even when she was in the competition? Hadn't she denied that, with each level that she moved forward in *American Singing Star*, she'd moved further and further from herself, willingly trading her identity for fame and accolades? Hadn't she hidden who she really was in order to gain approval? In order to fit in? In order to be loved?

Today, Sam was meeting Cody's aunt and uncle and cousins. They were probably doing it right now.

How was it going? Was he going to be okay? What if he needed someone to talk to about it?

Who was she *really*?

The safest thing was to run away from him, to hide in these hills, possibly right up until his departure date. To go back to making the world all about herself: her pain, and her betrayals and her challenges, how unfair the world had been to her.

But had that preoccupation brought her one single thing to like about her life? Had it moved her any closer to a satisfying existence?

Her grandmother had always known who she was. And her Gram would tell her, in no uncertain terms, to go home to the beach cottage, and be strong enough to offer Sam exactly what he had seen in her.

Her compassion, her creativity, her sensitivity.

As she packed up her things and headed back to her car she felt as if this might be the bravest thing she had ever done. It felt as if she was honoring the person her grandmother had always known she was.

This was her lesson, her legacy from Gram. Bravery was not stepping out in front of a live audience of thousands and a TV audience of millions.

But bringing the gift of herself to another human being. Believing that she had a gift to offer. She missed her grandmother so much in that moment, and felt so grateful for her that Allie thought she might weep.

Cody and Sam had already returned from meeting the Australian relatives when she got back. Popsy greeted her as though she had been gone for years instead of hours. Was it her imagination or was Popsy more lively?

Even with Cody having his nap, and Sam with his feet up on the back deck, her house felt *full* in ways it had not felt before they had arrived in her life. Taking a deep breath, ordering herself to be brave, Allie grabbed a water and joined him on the deck.

"Hey." She suddenly felt shy, and wondered if she was intruding.

Do not look at his lips.

She looked. Good grief, he was gorgeous.

But he nudged a chair with his foot, an invitation, a confirmation she had done the right thing. She took it.

"How did the family reunion go?" she asked.

"Actually, really well. The whole family has this kind of laid-back vibe. We built sandcastles on the beach. I took verbal orders from two pint-size people, and hand signals from another. Tears from all as the tide came in and swept it all away. Nap time."

"Are you okay?"

"Oh, sure. Why wouldn't I be?"

"I don't know. You look...pensive."

Actually, *sad* would have said it much, much better.

"The little girl, Nicole, just took Cody under her wing as if she was a mother hen. Bossing him around, playing with him, teasing him, teaching him little songs, ignoring the fact he didn't sing one word back to her. There was a kind of instant connection between him and both those kids."

"Cousins," she said. "They often have those bonds."

"Do they? Is this from your expertise file on early childhood development?" There was an edge to his voice.

"Did Cody seem happy with them in a way he isn't with you?" Allie asked with soft caution.

"I *want* his happiness," he snapped.

"Tell me what happened, Sam." She realized that he was trying to hide the sadness from her, that he didn't know it was so apparent in the lines of his face.

He looked at her as if he was going to tell her to go to hell, and then he ran his fingers through the dark waves of his hair, looked out to sea and looked back at her. Debating.

When he spoke, his voice low and pained, she realized she had stopped breathing, recognizing this as another pivotal moment.

He would trust her with his deeper self, or he wouldn't.

"Bill is so much like my brother-in-law, Adam, that it hurts. You think the ragged edge has come off grieving and then, there it is."

"They look alike?"

"It's that, but it's more. So much more. The accent, the humor, the way of *being*. Adam was my best friend. I met him when I was just starting my company. He came to work for me. I introduced him to my sister."

He smiled, possibly the saddest smile Allie had ever seen. "I used to call him a dumb Aussie. He was the greatest guy I ever knew. Losing one of them would have been more than I could bear, but both? If it wasn't for Cody, I don't know how I would have continued to get up every day.

"But I look at that poor kid, and I think, if it's doing this to me, a full-grown man, supposedly with a few coping skills for life, what's it doing to him?"

He took in a long, ragged breath. "Cody took to Bill immediately. And the cousins. And you are probably very right. Seeing him with a family—a real family—made me aware of all the things I haven't been able to give him. I do want his happiness. I want it with all my heart. I just wish more of it came from being with me."

She contemplated that. And then she said, "You know what I see when he is with you? You are his rock. In a world that has shown him it is not always safe, you are his safe place. The place where it's okay for him to grieve in whatever way his three-year-old self needs to grieve.

He doesn't feel pressured to be happy around you, to talk, to meet your needs. He knows you are the adult and it's your job to meet his needs. He trusts you completely. He knows you are in this together. And you are so sure that he saw his father in his father's brother, Bill. Of course he did.

"But don't you think he sees his mother in you? Every single day?"

"I doubt that. We looked like we came from different parents. She's the one Cody got all those blond curls from."

But I bet he got those soulful liquid-brown eyes straight from your family line, Allie thought.

"It's not so much about looks," Allie said, slowly. "Though I'm sure you have resemblances to your family you are not aware of. And mannerisms. Like Bill has some of the same quirks as Adam, I bet you, unknowingly, have some of your sister's. Maybe the way you tilt your head when you listen, or the way you throw back your head to laugh."

Oops, letting him know she was observing him way too closely, but getting Sam to hear this seemed far more important than protecting herself.

"I'd be willing to bet," she continued, "that you shared a value system with your sister, a kind of bone-deep decency, a courage for facing life, a determination that Cody sees in you every day, and is reassured by."

"Stop it," Sam growled, "you are going to make me choke up. Very unmanly."

Allie was gratified by the spark being back in his voice, gratified that somehow she had stumbled on just the right words. "Go ahead. Cry. As if there could be enough tears."

"To be honest? I don't think I have any left."

This was exactly why she had come back from her hike, some instinct—or perhaps all that was best about Gram alive in her—drawing her here, to where she was needed. She didn't say anything. She just sat with him, the silence comfortable between them as they watched the waves in the distance, and the crowds on the beach.

Children playing in the sand, teenagers shoving each other near the water's edge, women who had undone the back strap of their bathing suit tops, shirtless guys throwing footballs and posturing for those women who pretended not to see them. There were sounds, waves crashing, and birds cawing and shouts and laughter, mommies calling after their children.

Life, really. Ordinary life, unfolding before them on the beach. A simple scene that was so reminiscent of the kind of happy, carefree days of lighthearted spirit that summer brings.

"They've got a full day planned tomorrow," Sam said, breaking the comfortable silence between them. "They're quite excited about being here in the States for the Fourth of July celebrations. There's a parade on Main Street in the morning, some kind of festival after, and then fireworks on the beach tomorrow night."

"I always wanted to be here for Fourth of July," she said. "But that was always the week my grandmother went away to visit my great-aunt Mildred. I usually came toward the end of the summer, when my mother needed to get ready for the fall semester. I can't even tell you what coming here meant. Such a sense of being accepted, of being home, of being loved."

Allie sighed. "I miss her so much."

He looked at her. "You should come with us."

"Me? Why?"

"Because you'll be missing your grandmother. It feels like one of those family celebration kind of days that you should share with someone."

"Do you feel sorry for me?" she asked, appalled she had let her wistfulness for those days with her grandmother be so apparent. "Because of what I told you about missing Gram?"

"I don't think I would have said I felt sorry for you. It's just that I know what it's like to miss people."

He actually ducked his head, looking faintly embarrassed. She realized, stunned, he felt *connected* to her. He *wanted* to share the day with her.

"I thought you weren't anxious to have them meet me," she reminded him, worried he would regret acting on this momentary connection brought on by shared confidences. "Your roommate."

"Okay. Maybe you should forego the red bikini."

She realized he was teasing her. It felt strangely and gloriously intimate. She gave him a little punch on the arm.

He pretended to be hurt. "Just for the parade part!"

"Okay. I'll wear my black one instead."

He threw back his head and laughed. The sun hit the column of his throat, and his laughter rang down the beach.

That felt strangely and gloriously intimate, also.

"No, seriously, come," Sam said. "After spending the day with them, they just don't seem like the type to jump to judgment. Plus, anybody who knew you for more than ten minutes would know how decent you are."

She snorted. "At last count about two point four million people would disagree with you."

He was silent for a moment, and then his voice low, he admitted, "I watched one of the *American Singing Star* videos last night. Part of it."

She froze and stared at him.

"After you told me about it, I wanted to see for myself. You didn't even look like you." His eyes went to her hair.

She touched it self-consciously. Sometimes she was still shocked by how short it was. "This is my natural color. But they already had a blonde. So, they suggested one of us dye our hair so the audience would have no problem differentiating us. I'd like to say we picked straws, but eager-to-please me just wagged my hand in the air."

"It was so long."

"It was long, but not that long. Extensions," she said. "They had stylists who did it all. Hair, makeup, outfit selection."

"I'm somehow reassured that you didn't pick that outfit for yourself. I just don't see you as a black leather kind of girl."

His simple statement made her feel validated in some way. While she had been growing increasingly uncomfortable with her talent show transformation, every single person she knew had gushed about it.

"I didn't pick the song, either. *Everything*

was choreographed. Even—" she heard the faint bitterness in her voice "—a romance."

"I'm glad you weren't seduced by it. I'm glad it ended in a way that made it so you would never want to go back. All that phoniness would have killed you."

His words washed over her. For a blinding moment Allie stood in the truth. She had seen that show as the triggering event in a landslide of losses: her career, her love, her dignity.

But in Sam's simple words, for the first time, she understood what the real loss had been.

She had lost herself.

"You in black leather," Sam said with a dismayed shake of his head. "So wrong."

It felt as if she needed to keep the enormity of her discovery to herself. She kept her tone light. "You haven't seen the black bikini yet!"

He laughed again, but then grew serious. "Those people? All two point four million of them? They didn't know *you* at all."

She realized, looking back on that period of her life, she didn't know who she was, either. So eager to please, so eager to gain the prize they held out for her, so sure somehow the *real* her could not accomplish that, a belief they had underscored with every request: change this, wear that, try this song.

She saw now that it wasn't necessarily money.

Or fame.

It was approval they had held out to her.

And then snatched away.

"You should come tomorrow," he said softly. "Bill and Kathy seem to know a whole lot about having wholesome family fun. When's the last time you did that?"

"Wouldn't that involve having a wholesome family?"

He laughed. "Come. Have fun."

Quit hiding.

But hiding was oh, so safe. The last time she'd gone way out of her comfort zone, she'd auditioned for the show. With disastrous consequences, she reminded herself. It had been the end of her "wholesome" family dream, the one he had so clearly seen in the mist around her, the picture of picket fences and baby carriages.

What if a day spent like this triggered all those longings she had set aside?

But suddenly the appeal of spending a fun-filled day with him and his makeshift family was too much to resist.

Suddenly she saw herself as way too introspective, too serious, too safe. He wasn't asking her to marry him and help him raise Cody. He wasn't asking her to adopt his Australian family as her own.

He was suggesting she get out and have some

good old Fourth of July fun: parades, ice cream, hot dogs, flags, fireworks.

What could be more wholesome—and harmless—than that? Besides, what would her grandmother tell her to do? She could almost feel Mavis giving her a little push toward Sam.

"Okay," she said.

It felt as if she was closing her eyes and stepping off a high diving board.

But it felt as if *she* was doing it: the real Allie, not some imposter whose whole life had been created to gain ratings on a television show.

CHAPTER TWELVE

"YOU'RE TOUCHING POOPERMAN'S CAPE," Sam said the next morning, aghast. He had come into the kitchen to find Allie hunched over the table.

"Pooperman's cape?" She glanced up at him, a needle in her hands.

He was pretty sure she was in her pajamas. The outfit was not what you would call sexy—it looked like she was wearing a man's shirt, that was rolled up bulkily around her arms, and ended above her knees.

But the shirt had fallen off one shoulder, and her legs were totally exposed and undeniably gorgeous.

Somehow the shirt was more sexy than the damned bathing suit.

Or maybe sexy was the way she was looking at him, her tongue caught between her teeth, her eyes luminous.

The cape in question was spread across her

lap, a needle and thread in her hands. There was a pair of scissors there.

Sam had to fight an itch to pick up the scissors, and cut those black tips out of her hair—what remained of *Tempest*.

"That's what Adam and I called his cape. You can't touch it. I have to sneak it into the laundry when Cody is sleeping."

"I just added an American flag lining to it, for the parade. We can take it out again after."

"You can't add things to Pooperman's cape!"

"It loses its magical powers?" she said drily.

"You have no idea what you are playing with," Sam said. But looking at her, sitting there, so adorable in her men's shirt and messy hair and bare feet, he wondered which of them had no idea what they were playing with. Had he really invited her to spend the day with them?

"I can take the lining out in a jiffy if it upsets Cody."

There was a neat stack of flag-patterned squares beside her.

"And what's this?" he asked, picking up the top square. The square unfolded into another cape. He frowned. "You're not expecting me to wear one, are you?"

She gave him a disparaging look, as if she had already figured out he was too much of a poor sport to play along. Why would he feel vaguely insulted by that?

"I made one for each of the kids." She looked away, and said, softly, as if she didn't want him to think she was an idiot, "And one for Popsy, too."

He stared at her. "Were you up all night?" he finally asked.

"Just half of it."

"Who has this kind of stuff on hand?" he asked, incredulously. "Like what? Fifty yards of American flag material?"

"My grandmother was a quilter. There's tons of fabric here. She taught me how to sew when I was just little. It reminds me of her, in the nicest way, when I sew."

Sam looked at the perfect little stack of capes, and at the look on her face. It was that luminescent look again, her eyes shining, a contented little smile drifting across the plumpness of her bottom lip.

It occurred to him that Allie was excited for the day. Isn't that what he'd wanted when he convinced her to come? To get her to reengage in life, instead of hiding? He wanted her to let go of the notion she was the one who had something to be ashamed of over the whole *American Singing Star* fiasco.

Still, there was something about the enthusiasm in her that was a little dangerous.

"You can't just add stuff to Pooperman's
cape," Sam said again, just to make sure she
knew there were rules that couldn't be ignored.

"Sorry, I didn't know." She didn't sound very
sorry. Well, she hadn't seen one of the famous
meltdowns.

Come to think of it, there still hadn't been
any famous meltdowns. Not since they'd arrived. That had to be a record. That would
probably all change when Cody awoke to find
his cape was not only not within reach, but had
been altered.

On cue, Cody came out of his bedroom,
rubbing sleep from his eyes. Astonishingly,
he seemed not to notice his cape had not been
on the floor beside his bed this morning. He
stopped when he saw them at the kitchen table
with the cape in between them.

Allie flipped the cape off the table and went
and sank down on her heels in front of him.
"Look," she said, "I added something to your
cape just for today. And I made Popsy a matching one!"

With a flourish she put the cape around his
shoulders. And then she called the dog and put
the matching cape on him.

The two of them—make that all three of them—stood frozen, looking at her in disbelief.

"You look amazing," she declared.

Cody looked to Sam for reaction.

"Like you could vanquish evil with a simple wave of your hand. And paw," Sam said solemnly.

Cody obviously had no idea what *vanquish* meant, and probably not *evil*, either, but he fingered the shiny new lining of the cape, deciding. Then he smiled. It looked as though he was pretty sure he had been bestowed with a superpower he had not possessed before.

"Allie made Nicole and Bryan capes, too," Sam said, and that was the final reassurance Cody needed. He smile deepened to a happy boyish grin, and he spread his arms like a plane and flew out the back door onto the deck, with Popsy on his heels. Their rambunctious running around the deck made the whole house vibrate.

"Did we just dodge a bullet?" Allie asked.

"We did, but that's nothing for a family of superheroes."

A light went on in her face, at the word *family*. That was a bit of a mistake to make it sound as if they—him and her and Cody and Popsy—were family. But still, Sam faced the truth about his invitation. It wasn't just about getting her out of hiding, assuaging some pain that had stolen her dreams from her.

Somehow, he wanted her to know that those dreams, the ones she had sworn she had given up on, were attainable.

Staying up all night to make the capes was a perfect example of the kind of life she yearned for and was suited for: dogs and kids and costumes. Family. Fun. Laughter.

Sam, of course, knew he was the worst possible person to be letting anyone know their dreams were attainable.

Especially wholesome, garden-variety kinds of dreams.

But Kathy and Bill, with their somehow perfectly imperfect little family, could show Allie how it could be. They could give her hope. He was certain of that.

He practically herded them all out the door and down the beach, as if he could reassign some of the responsibility he had taken on to others.

And from the moment they all met, Sam felt the relief of a plan going well. Nicole and Bryan made a fuss over Cody in his flag cape, and then threw themselves on Popsy, squealing even more about the almost unbearable cuteness of the dog in a cape. Popsy lapped it all up, while Cody looked pleased as punch to be the owner of such a marvel of a beast.

With a certain endearing shyness, Allie gave Nicole and Bryan their capes, too. Their eyes went round with the wonder of it. Soon the excitement had reached such levels that Kathy kicked them all—children and dog— out on the deck and shut the door firmly behind them.

"What a wonderful gift," Kathy said, and looked askance at Sam. He realized in all the hoopla of the cape presentations, he had not made introductions.

"This is Allie," Sam said. "She's my—"

He hesitated. Only a few days had gone by. How had she come to be so much? His roommate. Confidante.

"Landlady," he said, taking the safest route.

"You can't be a landlady," Kathy said, eyeing Allie after introductions. "You are much too young for that."

"Accidental landlady," Allie said, and explained briefly about the mix-up.

"Did you make those precious capes for everyone?" Kathy asked, apparently not finding their living arrangement worthy of any more attention.

"You don't think I made them?" Sam asked.

They all laughed at that.

"Yes," Allie said shyly.

"They are so adorable," Kathy said.

"Not too loud," Sam warned her. "Cody does not want to be adorable. I don't think Popsy does, either. Superheroes are not adorable."

And then all the adults were laughing again, with a kind of ease, and Sam felt as if they had all known each other for a long time.

It soon became evident Bill and Kathy *loved* Allie. As they walked to the parade, Kathy and Allie talked easily. And Nicole, Bryan and Cody took turns squabbling over who got to hold the dog's leash and who got to hold Allie's hand. Well, what wasn't to love about someone who arrived with a child and a dog and all-American superhero capes?

Allie's initial shyness dissipated rapidly and she fit seamlessly into the lovely dynamic of this family. It was evident to him that Allie was a girl who needed to be loved. Who would thrive on it. Who would come into herself.

He wondered if he was playing with fire encouraging this transformation of Allie.

But as he stood beside her at the parade, looking at her shining face, he decided it was worth the risk.

This was what he was aware of since arriving at the beach. Basically, he'd been alone with the enormity of his grief, with the enormity of leaving his carefree bachelor days behind and becoming a parent.

That was not to say people had not been around him and that sympathy had not been plentiful. His coworkers, his staff in particular, shared his grief. Adam had belonged to all of them, after all.

And yet, the huge emptiness of his new world Sam carried alone.

The insecurity he felt about Cody, he carried alone.

Allie made him feel not alone with it, as if the touch of her hand, and the look in her eyes, the way she listened, took some burden from it, made it lighter.

He made Cody surrender Popsy's leash to his cousins, then lifted him up on his shoulders so that he could see the parade better.

And felt the shine of the moment as the parade started and the children squealed with delight and excitement as the clowns danced out in front of them, passing out candy to the crowds.

They were followed by a band and cheerleaders doing amazing gymnastics. Then a wagon pulled by a pair of donkeys, who appeared indifferent to the local fire engine that followed them, sirens blaring.

The floats came next, from wonderful, like Fun Florist, to almost embarrassingly bad,

Phil's Steakhouse. That float was blaring some awful song about *so delicious you can't miss us*, and had a man dressed as a large steak waving at the crowd.

"Did *miss* really become *mish*? You can't *mish* us?" Allie groaned and buried her face in her hands.

"Look at it this way," he said, "you can't do worse."

"My fear is maybe I can."

He put his hand around her shoulder, reassuringly. He squeezed. He should have let go. But somehow, one hand stayed holding Cody steady on his shoulder, and one stayed around Allie. She beamed up at him.

There had been so little happiness. What could it hurt to give himself and his nephew over to the day? To the days they had left here at Sugar Cone Beach?

Before he had to make a terrible decision about what was best for everyone involved, even if it left him more alone than he had ever been in his entire life.

Sam pushed that thought from his mind. Just for today he would be carefree in a way that he thought would never be possible again.

Allie was not sure when—if ever—she had experienced such a perfect day. When the parade ended, they joined the crowds that went to the street fair. People stopped them to admire the kids' American flag Superman capes and to pet the dog. They had their faces painted, and they ate hot dogs. The kids all had red, white and blue candy floss.

Bill and Sam became quite competitive throwing baseballs at a target. Bill won a huge stuffed bear which he gave not to Nicole who wanted it, but to Kathy. There was something about the way they looked at each other in that brief moment that made Allie feel all squishy inside.

And then Sam won the same bear, and gave it not to Cody, but to Allie.

Of course, she told herself, it was probably because Cody already had his hands full with the dog's leash, and the bear was too big for him to carry anyway.

Still, there was something about a man winning a stuffed animal for you at the fair that was part of a perfect all-American dream and all-American day. And she felt even squishier inside.

The children turned the corner from happy to cranky in the blink of an eye, and they walked back through the July heat and the packed streets to Bill and Kathy's rental.

The beachfront rental could have been intimidatingly posh and a reminder of the life Allie had so briefly glimpsed with lots of glass and steel and marble, but somehow the glamour of it was overridden by flip-flops in various sizes at the door, toys out, colorful beach towels, children's books in leaning stacks.

Somehow, Bill and Kathy had, without trying, given the place a sense of *home*. Anticipating a struggle to separate children, Kathy just put mats on the living room floor, and the kids all flopped down together. Nicole and Bryan protested, crabbily, they weren't at all tired.

They were given the stuffed bears to sleep with, and then, still muttering protests, Cody tucked under one of Nicole's protective arms, one bear tucked under the other, and Popsy tucked under his.

As if it was second nature to him, Allie watched as Sam leaned into the heap of sleeping children, the dog and the huge stuffed bears, and gently loosened all the cape strings from around sweaty little necks.

"I should go," Allie said, feeling suddenly as if she had overstayed her welcome, as if they were all family, and she was not. An interloper somehow. The adults would want to relax, they would want to read books or snooze in the sun. Her perfect day was over.

"Nonsense," Kathy said. "The monsters are sleeping." *Monsters* was said with an abundance of affection. "It's our turn. The guys can have a beer, and you and I will have a glass of wine and put up our feet. I've bought shrimp to put on the barbie tonight, and I've heard this is a great place to watch the fireworks from. There's a fire pit built into the deck. Let's make a day of it, shall we?"

Really, she should have insisted on going home.

But Allie was not strong enough to pull away from the circle of warmth she found herself in.

And so she sat on a lounger, with a crisp glass of white wine in her hand, watching as Sam and Bill, now shirtless and shoeless, threw a football back and forth on the beach.

Their voices floated up to the women: masculine, laced with laughter. Were they showing off just a bit, just as they had been when they won the teddy bears?

"Ah," Kathy said, watching them, "I can't tell you how good this moment is for my heart. I wondered if either of them would ever let themselves have moments like this again."

"It's been a terrible blow to all of you," Allie said. She looked over at Kathy. She saw a tear sliding down her face as Bill leaped high in the air to catch a ball Sam had deliberately made nearly impossible to catch.

"Life is beautiful, isn't it?" Kathy asked softly. "And sad, and hard and heartbreaking. And then, beautiful all over again."

Allie suddenly saw her own life in a different light, and realized how true Kathy's words were.

The talk between them turned lighter, a universal language between women. They discussed the latest book of an Australian author they both liked, and movies they had enjoyed, which actors made them swoon.

The children woke up, and the guys took them swimming, and Kathy and Allie got salads ready, and finally, as it got dark, put shrimp on the barbecue.

After a fabulous grilled dinner, they took lawn chairs onto the beach, joining the crowds of people there. Somehow, Sam was beside Allie, and they oohed and ahhed as much as the children. She could feel him there, a scent coming off his sun-warmed skin, his presence making the warm evening and the explosions of light, the effect doubled as they reflected in black water, absolutely and utterly enchanting.

At the first explosion, Popsy came out from under Sam's chair and leaped on Allie's lap. She watched Sam's hand play in the dog's fur, and felt a tickle of desire, completely inappropriate for such a family-friendly event.

After, they retreated to the deck of the rental, with its built-in fire pit. Allie felt as if everything was fading, save Sam and her awareness of him.

The way he looked, the way he laughed, the way he was in the world. He teased the kids, talked to his brother-in-law, tickled the dog's ears, looked after the fire, supervised Cody, who had discovered the delight of swirling a red-tipped stick, fresh from the fire, against the night sky.

Each of those small things spoke to who he was: so strong, so sure of himself, so able to be himself in the world, whether he was aware of that or not.

She watched as he knelt beside Cody, whispered in his ear, hugged him briefly and tightly against his chest.

This is a good man, Allie found herself thinking. The feeling she had for him was so strong, she felt that desire, once again, to leave, to run away, to hide.

To protect herself from something that had hurt her before and could hurt her again. Looking back on the whole day, it filled her with a sense of longing.

Yearning.

She had a little war going on with herself. She needed to leave. She needed to stay. She needed to be cautious. She needed to be bold.

Kathy brought out a guitar. "This was in the unit," she said. "Does anybody play?"

CHAPTER THIRTEEN

"ALLIE DOES," SAM said softly.

For a moment Allie felt a sense of betrayal. She had told Sam she didn't sing publicly anymore. Still, this wasn't *really* publicly. Just a small family gathering.

Hesitantly, Allie took the instrument Kathy held out to her. It was a cheap guitar and badly out of tune, but she fiddled with the frets, and then finally, she strummed a few tentative notes.

The strange thing was she barely knew these people, and yet the fear of judgment that had filled her since *American Singing Star* was absent. In fact, having the guitar in her hands, people around her, the fire glowing, made her feel as at home as she had ever felt with a guitar.

She suddenly realized she was not in a war with herself, at all. The decision wasn't whether to leave or stay, to be cautious or bold.

The decision was whether or not to be herself. Whether or not to come home to herself.

"Okay," she said to the children. "I'm going to teach you how to sing in the round. You, too," she said to the adults. She went around the circle and numbered everyone, including Cody so he wouldn't feel left out, though obviously he would not be singing the rounds.

"One, two, one, two," she sang out. "All the ones, over here, all the twos over there."

"I forget which number I am," Sam said devilishly, and Nicole and Bryan yelled at him he was a two.

"This is the song," Allie said, "I'll sing it, and then we'll sing it all together. 'Flames are climbing, flames are climbing, come closer, come closer, In the glowing, in the glowing, Come sing with us and be joyous.' Is everybody ready?"

No one answered.

"What?" she asked.

"I think you may have the most beautiful voice I've ever heard," Kathy said. "Ever."

Allie blushed and dropped her head, but not before she saw that Sam was looking at her, and he was smiling.

As if he was proud of her. As if he had deliberately put an obstacle in front of her that he knew she could overcome. As if he saw the truth of her, and knew she had allowed her true self to come out.

Reading too much into it, she scolded herself. But she nodded at him.

"Sing," she said, and their voices rose together, riding the sparks into the night until it felt as though they were touching the stars.

As she played the guitar and sang, some of the neighboring families wandered over and were invited to stay. A sense of community leaped up.

They sang everything: children's songs and ballads. They sang rock and roll and theme songs from television shows. Sometimes the singing was good, and mostly it was terrible. Sometimes they could remember all the words and all the verses of each song but mostly they could not.

And as the night wore on, the songs became quieter and quieter. One by one the children nodded off to sleep, Bryan in his mother's arms, Nicole in her father's, Cody in Sam's.

Her awareness of Sam, of his basic goodness and strength, his willingness to do the right thing, intensified every time she looked over at him and saw that child nestled so trustingly into his chest, fast asleep.

Allie was not sure she had ever enjoyed using her voice as much as she did leading a singalong, long into the night, on the Fourth of July at Sugar Cone Beach.

Finally, though, her voice was nearly gone, and she set the guitar down.

"One more?" Sam asked. "Please?

She realized she could refuse him nothing. They had known each other such a short time. How could she feel so strongly toward him? She reached for the guitar.

"Could we finish with this?" Sam asked. "It's a song my brother-in-law insisted I learn every word to."

His voice, a beautiful, rich, natural tenor rose, alone, into the night, as he sang the opening bars of "Waltzing Matilda."

One by one other voices joined Sam's. Allie picked up the song easily and accompanied on the guitar, but found herself so choked up she could barely sing.

Their voices rose and became one, until they were all Australians, and all Americans, and all part of that amazing beauty and sadness and heartbreak and then beauty again that is to be human.

The impromptu party broke up shortly after, neighbors—new friends—gathering their sleepy children and calling their goodbyes.

"What a splendid evening," Kathy said, as Allie and Sam organized Cody and Popsy for a walk up the darkened beach to their own place.

"You really have an incredible voice," Bill

said. "I have a friend, in Australia, who is a record producer. Do you think—"

"No," Allie said quickly.

She couldn't follow that dream again. She just couldn't.

Sam seemed to understand. He nestled the sleeping Cody up on his shoulder and took her hand.

Together they walked out into the sand and the night. He didn't let go of her hand, presumably because it was dark, the silence companionable between them.

At the cottage, they stood outside for a minute before going in. The night was velvety warm, an embrace of stars and sea-scented water.

"Thank you for a beautiful day," Allie said huskily.

"No, thank you."

They stood there for a moment, as if both of them knew the perfect way to end a perfect day.

His eyes dark with yearning, Sam leaned toward her.

Wanting something from him that she had never wanted so much from another human being—more than a kiss, but connection— Allie leaned toward him.

But then Popsy pulled on his leash, wanting his bed, and Cody woke suddenly, and the moment was gone.

In her empty bedroom, by herself, listening to the sounds of Sam getting an uncooperative sleepyhead into his pajamas, she wasn't sure if it was a good thing or a bad thing that they had pulled back.

She did know she had experienced a near miss of a kiss. And she ached for the thing that had not happened.

Sam awoke in the morning, aware of three things: one, it was raining, a steady drum on the tin roof. Two, somewhere—probably in the kitchen—Allie was singing about how rare rain was in California. And three, that feeling he had woken with for eight solid months, that feeling of being in a black hole of despair, was gone.

Replaced, not quite with lightness, but with a cautious sense that maybe, just maybe, everything would be okay.

Did you fight a feeling like that? Or surrender to it?

Somehow, he had intended the day, yesterday, to be a gift to Allie. A message. *See? Life can be good. You can believe dreams come true. You can miss your grandmother, but still live life.*

But maybe it was the nature of gifts that the giver received as much as the recipient. Whether they were ready or not.

From the nest of his bed, Sam heard a knock on the back door.

"Is it too early?"

He recognized Nicole's voice, looked at the clock beside his bed, and was surprised by how late he had slept.

"We've brought breakfast," Kathy sang out. "And rainy day things. Board games. A movie."

Allie said something about the rain spoiling their vacation.

"We *love* rain," Nicole pronounced.

"Why do you love rain?" Allie asked.

"Well, first," Nicole answered, "because we don't get very much where we live, but second, it makes me like the sunny days even better!"

Rain makes you like the sunny days.

Way too deep, Sam chastised himself, when he started contemplating that. He got up out of bed, pulled on a T-shirt and some shorts and padded to the kitchen. He stood in the doorway for a moment, looking at them.

He hadn't realized Cody was up. He and Allie had been drawing pictures with crayons on a huge piece of newsprint spread out on the kitchen table.

Now the tiny kitchen was crowded, and yet somehow there was room for everyone around that table.

"Uncle Sam," Nicole said, "do you know how

to draw a unicorn?" She was holding out a green crayon to him.

When had he become "uncle"? He hadn't really noticed. *His family,* he thought, stunned that he had a family again.

Stunned, and a tiny bit frightened. What had more potential to hurt than this?

He scowled at Nicole. "Don't be ridiculous," he said, scorning the crayon she held out. "Everyone knows unicorns are purple."

"Are they, Auntie Allie?" Nicole asked.

Sam looked at her. Allie was wearing one of her many I-lost-a-ton-of-weight-at-the-spa outfits. Faded blue T-shirt and sweatpants in the very same horrible shade.

She hadn't combed her hair yet, and it was sticking up all over.

She was so cute it took his breath away.

So, Allie was family, too. How could that possibly feel so right after such a short length of time?

As the rain pattered on the tin roof of the cottage, he pulled up a chair and searched through the crayons.

He added a purple unicorn to the unfolding mural.

Allie came over, and put her hand on his shoulder as she leaned over it to look. She leaned over him harder as she took the crayon from his hand, and made an adjustment to the horn.

Everything else in the room seemed to fade. Just her, touching him, filling his senses with her smell.

Somehow, everything felt so right. After that, the day unfolded with a delicious sense of endlessness.

They drew pictures and played games. They ate peanut butter sandwiches for lunch, and then defied the rain and went outside and jumped in puddles and swam in the ocean.

After, they came in soaked, and the whole house soon reeked of wet dog. Kathy went home and got a change of clothes for them all, and Nicole had a hot shower and the boys shared a hot bath together. They watched a movie. They built extravagant blanket forts in the living room. They ordered pizzas for dinner.

Sam noticed that, like him, Cody seemed to have turned a page. There was a lightness about him that had not been there when they had arrived at the beach. He had a willingness to engage.

And Allie! Ever since she had leaned over him this morning, it was as if everything else was just a backdrop to her: to her shining eyes, to her ocean-slicked hair, to her laughter, to her willingness to get down on the floor and play.

Nobody wanted the day to end.

He felt Nicole tugging on his sleeve.

"Can Cody come for a sleepover at our house tonight?"

It felt as if his world went strangely still. His world had been he and Cody for so long. They had not been apart for one hour since it had happened, let alone a whole night.

What if something happened?

What if he let Cody out of his sight, and something bad happened? What if they didn't watch him closely enough and he wandered onto the beach? What if a fire started? Or that burglar broke into their house while he wasn't there to protect Cody?

He knew these doubts were ridiculous. Kathy and Bill had managed not just to keep their children from harm, but to shape them into wonderful people. Creative, moving toward independence, sure of themselves.

Their children were speaking, a mean-spirited voice inside him pointed out.

He understood he was grappling with a bigger question.

What if he lost Cody, too?

"Please, Uncle, please, please, please?" Bryan joined the chorus.

CHAPTER FOURTEEN

ALLIE FELT SAM stiffen at Nicole's innocent question.

Kathy must have felt something, too. "Sleepovers!" she exclaimed. "I'm afraid they are all the rage among the six-year-old set."

"What exactly is a sleepover?" Sam asked.

"Oh, they're *soooo* good," Nicole said. "You watch movies, and dance to music, and talk *soooo* much. We might make popcorn or have another fire. Cody would love it!"

Cody looked up from his pizza.

"Wouldn't you love it, Cody?" Nicole asked.

Cody nodded, uncertainly at first, and then with enthusiasm.

"It's really Sam's decision," Kathy said firmly. "Nicole, it's been a long day."

"You want to go, buddy?" Sam asked.

Cody nodded. Though the truth was he seemed in shock as his things were packed up and he headed out the door.

At the last minute, he sat down furiously, shaking his head. He'd changed his mind. Allie shot Sam a look.

Did he look relieved?

"He wants the doggie," Nicole decided, and sure enough as soon as Popsy was included in the invitation, Cody got up off the floor, put his hand in Nicole's and trundled out the door.

"I'll call you," Kathy told Sam quietly, laying her hand on his shoulder. "If he changes his mind, or there are any kinds of problems, I'll call."

She obviously knew something momentous was happening. Then they were gone, and the house fell into sudden silence.

Allie knew, after a day like today, and a day like yesterday, there was a kind of danger in being alone together.

And yet how could you possibly leave a man with that look on his face to struggle through his challenges alone?

"What is it with Nicole?" he asked. "How does she know what Cody wants?"

"I'm afraid my early childhood education program didn't cover psychic abilities between children. Should we go sit on the deck for a bit?" she asked.

He looked as if he was going to say no, as if he knew she had detected a weakness in him, and as if his very survival depended on denying that weakness.

But he surrendered.

"Sure," he said, "let's go sit on the deck for a bit."

They sat, and then said, almost together, "It's so quiet."

"Quiet," Allie said, "but not empty somehow. It's as if the day, the laughter, has soaked into the walls and floorboards."

She had a sudden sense that when it was all over, when her life had gone back to normal, she was going to feel bereft.

"These were the kind of days you were made for," he proclaimed softly. "I knew it as soon as I saw you."

"After you got over thinking I was a wacko who killed old ladies, that is."

He rewarded her by laughing.

"And what about you?" she asked. "What about you and rainy days, and houses that are full of noise, and smell of wet dogs?"

"I don't know about *made* for it," he said. "Thrust into it."

"Nonsense. A man pushed into something against his own will would never build a fort that enthusiastically. Or draw such a stupendous purple unicorn."

"Is he going to be okay over there?" he asked softly.

She knew she could pull out her early childhood information and tell him how important it was for Cody to *differentiate*, to begin to see himself as separate from others, and that was probably particularly true in light of his loss, but that wasn't the real question. Not at all.

The real question was, was Sam going to be okay?

Somehow, even with the danger sizzling in the air between them, she needed to know the answer to that.

Or maybe, she had to be part of the answer to that.

The thought that was forming in her mind was terrifying. She sought refuge in her guitar. The notes flew out of it, snapping, floating, dancing like those sparks from the fire finding the night air.

"I should be working on Phil's Steakhouse," she said.

"That tune could sell a lot of steak," he said.

"Unfortunately, this tune is not Phil's Steakhouse. My guitar appears to be on strike when it comes to Phil."

"What is it then?"

She sang a rollicking little tune about mud

puddles and blanket forts and the sound of rainy days on the roof.

"You've found yourself, haven't you?" he asked quietly.

Had she? If she'd really found herself, didn't that have to extend to others? To him? Didn't she have to help him find himself, too? She could tell that the idea of Cody being away from him had left him feeling uneasy. He had given her this amazing gift of inviting her to experience family. What could she give him?

She set down the guitar. "We have the whole evening to ourselves. Let's be grown-ups," she suggested.

His eyes widened and he lifted an eyebrow wickedly at her.

She was not sure when she had become quite so comfortable with him, with his teasing, but she gave his arm a light punch.

"I mean, we're free. We don't even have the dog."

"Aren't you always free?" he asked her.

"I guess," she admitted, "though after that period where everyone recognized me, I got into a bit of a hermit habit. And I don't think I ever got back out." She could see the suggestion they do some grown-up things appealed to him much more once he determined it was also about her.

"Let's go to a movie," she said. "And maybe go for dinner after. We could be really wild. We could finish off the night with a drink."

Allie was aware she was holding her breath. It felt as if something important was being decided here. Earth-shattering. Because, really, no matter what she cloaked it in, her helping him, or him helping her, wasn't she asking him to go on a date?

"What movie?" he said, after a moment.

She felt the relief of his answer. "Anything but *Rugrats*."

"You don't even have a television. How can you be sick of *Rugrats*?"

"I can hear it when you play it on the computer. You know the walls in that cottage." In fact, she could hear *everything*, even the sound of him breathing.

He threw back his head and laughed, that beautiful, beautiful sound. "Agreed," he said.

Several minutes later, as she tried to decide what to wear, her nerve faltered. But then she threw on a sleeveless white top that showed off her tan and the arms toned from daily swimming, and a short, colorful, summery skirt that swished around her legs. She put on a light dusting of makeup, even though it was strictly against the cottage rules. She hadn't put on makeup since *American Singing Star*.

She put a straw fedora on. It covered the worst of her hair.

She looked in the mirror for a moment. She looked *cute*. There were little pink spots on her cheeks. Her eyes were shining.

What was she getting herself into? Too late. She was already in.

She deliberately brushed the thoughts away. It had been such a perfect few days. She was making new friends and moving out into the world again. She didn't need to analyze that endlessly. Wasn't there a whole philosophy about being in the moment? Couldn't she just do that?

There was no need to project into the future. Sam and Cody were here for a limited time, and it was counting down fast. There was no future.

Couldn't she just have fun? Couldn't she just be carefree, like those people who poured onto the beach in front of her house every day?

When she saw Sam's eyes widen with a certain male appreciation, Allie was glad for both the choice of makeup and the fun, flirty skirt. She might have even given it a little extra swish as they walked downtown to the theater together.

Still, it wasn't a date! It felt as if they scrupulously avoided it becoming a date, by avoiding holding hands.

Sugar Cone only had one theater, and it was playing an action thriller. There was a brief verbal scuffle at the wicket, when she talked about paying and Sam gave her an incredulous look. Then there was something lovely—and normal—about sitting in a darkened theater together. They didn't hold hands, but they shared a bucket of popcorn. Who knew fingers brushing over buttered popcorn could be so sexy?

"I'm starving," Sam said as they came out of the theater. They stood on the sidewalk together.

Allie was aware of an admiring glance he got from a woman passing by walking her dog. The woman smiled at him. Why did it melt something in Allie that Sam didn't even seem to notice?

"How can you be starving?" she teased him. "You ate a whole bucket of popcorn."

"I didn't eat a whole bucket. I wanted to, but you suggested sharing."

It was a tiny thing, really, going back and forth like this. And yet it felt unreasonably good to be with him. Maybe she had taken the whole hermit-hiding-out thing just a little too far.

"Phil's Steakhouse?" he deadpanned.

And then they were laughing together.

"I think a hamburger at Marty's Milkshakes is more in my price range."

"Your price range? You aren't paying."

"Well, I suggested this outing. So—"

"Is this why you suggested sharing popcorn? Because you were being frugal?"

"Why else?" she asked.

"I thought you were being romantic."

He was obviously teasing. She blushed.

"I'm your landlady. I think it's against the rules to be romantic with you."

He rocked back on his heels, and looked very much like a rebel who wanted to challenge the rules, but instead, he sighed. "Okay, now that you've established the rules, could we eat?"

"Someplace cheap," she said. "Dutch treat."

"Oh, be quiet," he said, and put his arm around her shoulder. "That place across the street looks good."

"That's the swankiest restaurant in town," she sputtered. She touched the brim of her fedora self-consciously. "I'm not dressed to go in there."

"It's a beach town," he said, unperturbed. "The dress code everywhere is casual. You impose a lot of rules on yourself, don't you?"

It occurred to her she did, her legacy from her mother. She decided, just for a little while, to leave the rules behind. Her Gram would approve of that!

"Just own it," Sam whispered in her ear, and gave the brim of her hat a little tug that made it feel like just possibly it could be seen as jaunty and stylish instead of a quick cover for a bad hair day.

The maître d' did not act as if there was anything wrong, at all, with what they were wearing. In fact, he gave them the best table in the house: a beautiful corner table on the patio, overlooking the sea.

"See?" Sam said. "I told you to own it. Look where it got us."

"That wasn't me. You're sending out the tycoon vibe," she whispered to him. "That's why we got the good table."

"Ha. Let me tell you how men think." He pretended his fingers were a meter. "Tycoon vibe, gorgeous legs, tycoon vibe, gorgeous legs." His finger meter went off the scale every time he said "gorgeous legs."

He thought she had gorgeous legs! That meant he'd looked. She could feel her confidence growing by the second.

That's what being with a man like him did. His confidence just rubbed off.

"Let's start with some calamari."

She looked at the price of it, and hid a gulp. When the waiter came he ordered a grotesquely expensive imported beer, and steak and lobster, the most expensive thing on the menu.

Was he showing off?

She cast him a look, and saw that he had not given his order a second thought. He'd simply ordered what he wanted.

"What are you having?" he asked her.

Old habits died hard. She could feel herself looking through the appetizers trying to find something inexpensive. He was paying, he'd already made that clear, but she couldn't make it feel as if she was taking advantage of him.

"Oh, for God's sake," he said as the waiter hovered. He took her menu from her and gave it back to the waiter. "Bring her the same."

"That's very controlling of you," she said, glaring at him.

"Think of it as masterful," he said with a wink.

"I can't eat that much," she protested. "And I think I've had enough butter for one evening."

He grinned at her. "There's no such thing as enough butter. And I'm hoping you can't finish, because then I'll get more."

His grin was so open and so mischievous— unconsciously charming—and she remembered her original goal. It was to keep his mind off Cody.

And it seemed to be working! What an unexpected bonus to see him looking happy and at ease.

And just like that, the moment of self-consciousness, of feeling somehow like she wasn't good enough for a place like this—or a guy like him—evaporated.

And they were just two people, doing what two people did. Getting to know each other.

What two people on their first date do, her mind insisted on telling her.

She took a sip of the beer that had arrived. "I had no idea beer could taste this good."

"Stick with the tycoons," he told her and lifted his glass to her. He came away with a deliberate foam moustache over his upper lip. It made her laugh.

She was not sure if anything had ever felt quite so wonderful as laughing with Sam Walker.

CHAPTER FIFTEEN

ALLIE BURIED HER upper lip in the foam, too, and made her own moustache. Then they were both laughing.

The food came.

"This is easily the most delicious thing I've ever eaten," she decided. She ate every bite, including all the butter.

"I saw crème brûlée on the menu. My favorite. I'm not sharing."

So two servings of crème brûlée arrived and the top was fired to golden, crunchy perfection right at their table.

"Am I in an episode of *Lifestyles of the Rich and Famous*?" she asked him, when the waiter had gone.

After dessert they sipped coffee, and she coaxed him to tell her about his business. He did, but then he turned pensive.

"I'm pretty driven. I like my work, a lot. Until Cody, it pretty much crowded out everything else."

"Maybe you just didn't find anything else you liked as much," she said.

"There really has been no room for anything else. My marriage was the first casualty."

"In what way?" She knew this hadn't just "come up." There was a warning in here. Enjoy everything he had to offer. Get attached to the stuff. But not him.

"I worked too much. She looked elsewhere."

His wife had had an affair? On Sam Walker? Looking at him, realizing how much he had come to mean to her, Allie found it difficult to believe. Worse, he seemed to think it was all his fault.

"That sounds like two people contributing equally to the demise of your marriage," she weighed in.

She actually felt she wanted to hit this woman she didn't know. How could anyone be so stupid? To be married to this man and step out on him?

"No, I take full responsibility."

He would, she thought, and yet he had made it pretty clear his wife had stepped out on him.

"She found someone new, and you are some-how responsible for that choice?" Allie pressed him.

"I got married, way too young, shortly after my parents died. It wouldn't take a genius to figure out I was trying to replace the sense of family I'd always had. But because I was so young, I felt I had to prove I could look after my wife. Not just look after her, but be the best at looking after her, the way my dad had been the best at looking after my mom. To me that meant being successful. Not just a little successful, a lot successful. Obsessed with successful, actually.

"Ironically, of course, since I thought I was doing everything for *us*, I pretty much neglected her. Long hours. Lots of traveling. She found someone who liked spending time with her. Who made her feel special. She stepped out. After we split up, she married him and got the life she always dreamed of, which, as it turned out, had nothing to do with having a great car or the best house on the block."

Allie hated her. "Sam, I'm sorry."

"I learned from it. Moved on."

Allie knew he was telling her exactly what he had learned from it. He was telling her not to pin any hopes on him. That steak and lobster and crème brûlée was all he was offering.

He was warning her he had priorities that did not involve a family.

"Cody has changed everything now, though, hasn't he?"

Something darkened in his eyes. It was not

just Cody that had changed everything, but the awareness of loss lurking around the corner, waiting to pounce.

"I've had to pull back, because of Cody, but thankfully, I've been developing a team of really good people for years. They've stepped up. The business is thriving despite the challenges of the last few months."

Sam realized it was getting late. He had lost track of the number of times the coffee cups had been filled.

Allie made him laugh. And talk about things he had not talked about before. He loved how she frowned at the menu, and felt uncomfortable, and then came into herself, and then felt uncomfortable again, and couldn't even begin to hide how the prices on the menu made her feel.

He liked spoiling her.

And he liked being a grown-up, too. But he thought he'd be glad when Cody was back, acting as a buffer between them.

His phone rang. Its ring tone was a very distinctive *boing, boing, boing.*

"Normally, I'd ignore," he said, "but it's Kathy and Bill." She nodded her understanding and he saw his own sudden concern mirrored in her eyes.

"Hello?"

"Uncle Sam?"

Again, he was not quite sure how he'd become Nicole's uncle, but he realized he had no objection to it.

"Is everything all right?"

"Yes."

"Then what are you doing up? It's very late."

"I have jet lag."

"Are you whispering?"

"I took my mum's phone and found your number in it. She told me I wasn't to bother you."

"It's no bother."

"We're going to the San Diego Zoo tomorrow. Cody really wants to come. Mum said I wasn't to ask you, though."

"Why's that?"

"She wouldn't say, but I think she thinks you're sad without Cody."

Sam closed his eyes. Is that how people perceived him? Leaning heavily on a three-year-old to meet his emotional needs?

"I do miss him," he said carefully, "but I'm not sad. Allie is taking care of me."

He looked across the table at her. She looked like that was news to her.

"So could he come with us tomorrow?"

"How do you know he wants to go with

you?" Did he really think a six-year-old was going to help him unlock the mystery of communicating with his three-year-old charge? If so, he was about to be disappointed.

"It's the *zoo*."

This was said as if he was an idiot.

"Okay. I agree. Cody would like the zoo."

"Could you make it seem like it was your idea?"

"How am I going to do that?" he asked. "I didn't even know you were going to the zoo."

"You'll think of something," Nicole proclaimed confidentially. "I'm so happy. I love Cody so much."

Those words, spoken by a child, made him feel choked up.

He hung up the phone. Allie could obviously piece together most of the conversation from hearing one side of it.

"It's good for him to be around other kids," Sam said when the look on Allie's face suggested that, like Kathy, she wondered if he was sad without Cody.

"Well, it looks like I'm in charge of looking after you," she said.

He needed to set her straight on that. He'd only said that because it seemed like a simple thing to say to assuage Nicole's fears for his well-being. He didn't need looking after because Cody had other plans. He had a million things he could do. Should do. He could drive into the office, for one.

Or drive, period. Drive down the road the way that car was meant to be driven when there was no three-year-old in his car seat. And no dog throwing up. It had been eight months since he'd had a drive like that.

So, he needed to set Allie straight.

That he didn't need her or anyone else looking after him. He never had.

Instead, he found himself smiling at her.

"More grown-up things?" he said hopefully.

She smiled back at him so angelically it filled him with suspicion. "Yes, but on my terms."

"What does that mean?"

"Free," she informed him.

"What have you got in mind?"

"There's free yoga on the beach every morning."

"I don't know about that."

"You'll love it," Allie told him.

"Women in stretch pants doing incredible things with their bodies," he said, conceding to her way too easily. "What's not to love?"

In the morning, he called Kathy, and asked, ever so casually, what their plans were for the day.

She told him they were planning an overnight trip to the San Diego Zoo and he suggested Cody might like to go.

"Are you sure?"

"It's the *zoo*," he assured her.

"You could come with us. And bring Allie."

Sometime during the night, he realized he had become quite attached to the idea of having some more time with Allie to himself.

"We've made some plans," he said, still ever so casual. "But I'll drop by with some stuff for Cody and make sure he's up for it."

"How about if we come your way? Popsy can't come to the zoo. He'll have to stay home. And we'll need to get a car seat from you."

The family arrived at the cottage in a flurry of activity, energy and superhero capes. Poor Popsy looked more than ready for a day without children, and crept off to Allie's bedroom.

Cody leaped into Sam's arms, took both cheeks in his pudgy hands, and regarded his uncle solemnly. Another one making sure *he* was all right.

"You want to go to the zoo, buddy?"

Cody nodded vigorously and squirmed down out of Sam's arms. He and Bryan spread their arms and zoomed around the kitchen while Nicole yelled instructions at them.

Kathy placed her hands over her ears, gave

him one long searching look, just like the one
Cody had just given him. Her gaze drifted to
Allie, and she gave a small nod, apparently sat-
isfied Sam would be well looked after.

He fetched the car seat out of his vehicle and
an overnight bag was organized for Cody. Then
he and Allie were alone in the house. It seemed
very quiet.

He was acutely aware of how great she
looked in yoga pants. If somebody would have
told him, a few days ago, that he would be looking forward to yoga on the beach, he would
have scoffed.

In fact, if they had told him he would be
looking forward to anything, he would have
scoffed.

And yet, here he was, walking through the
sand, carrying a yoga mat, with a beautiful
woman at his side, feeling as if spring had come
after a long, cold winter of darkness.

As it turned out, there was quite a lot not to
love about yoga on the beach. Allie had failed
to mention to him that the free, midmorning
class was attended mostly by middle-aged and
senior ladies who, whilst wearing yoga pants,
were not exactly filling them out the way he
had imagined.

Allie, who looked fantastic in the multicol-
ored stretch pants and large T-shirt she was

wearing, had placed herself where he couldn't see her.

Unless he really stretched—which, come to think of it, was the whole idea of yoga.

The teacher, a tyrant who seemed as if she had recently been released from her duties as prison guard or as a drill instructor for the marines, didn't approve of him stretching to try to catch a glimpse of Allie's downward facing dog. Or maybe she just didn't approve of him, specifically, or the entire male species, generally.

"She was mean," he told Allie after the class. They were sitting on their yoga mats, in the sand, in a shady area. He had his back braced against a tree, and his legs straight out in front of him. He took a tentative sip of some kind of green slime drink that Allie, in the spirit of keeping things free, had packed with her.

Allie's legs were still crossed in a serene lotus position. He felt like every muscle in his whole body was screaming.

"I've never thought she was mean," Allie said.

"Mr. Walker, press the perimeters of pain," he said, imitating her voice. "You're mean, too. A workout like that calls for a milkshake at the very least, and what are we drinking? Sludge."

"It's called Green Goddess. It's spinach and kale and celery. It's good for you."

"Nothing called Green Goddess is good for a man."

"Okay, yours is called Green Guy, then. And it's good for you."

"Why do those words always go hand in hand with something that tastes terrible? Like broccoli. Is there broccoli in this?"

He was making her laugh. He loved making her laugh.

After they finished their sludge, they walked back to the cottage. Allie was taking her job of keeping him entertained during Cody's absence very seriously. She dug old bikes from under the porch.

He eyed the one she offered to him suspiciously. "This seems rusty in all the wrong places."

"Don't be a chicken," she said. "I'll race you to the beginning of the bike path."

"I'm not fully recovered from yoga yet. And I'm lacking proper nourishment. And—"

She was on her bike and gone like a bolt of lightning. He wasn't just going to let her win!

He'd been right about the rust. The gears didn't work properly and he had to drag one foot on the ground to aid the mostly seized handbrake.

All of which turned out to be good. She beat him in the race. And he got the view he'd been vying for through an entire yoga class.

"I won," she crowed.

"I'm learning to be less competitive," he said.

Partway through the day, racing down a hill behind her, hearing her laughter, and feeling the thrill in his stomach from the speed, and her, and not knowing if he could stop, Sam was aware of something.

Despite the possible danger of crashing, he felt carefree.

Happiness had slipped in on him.

She stopped her bike. They were at a rocky outcrop that overlooked the ocean.

"Look," she breathed, "a whale."

But he didn't look at the whale. He looked at her face, radiating joy, and Sam Walker was filled with a sense of well-being.

"Race you home," she called as she took off again.

"You haven't got a hope," he yelled after her, knowing he didn't have the least bit of desire to wreck his view by getting in front of her. It was fun, though, to see her going as hard as she could, rising up on those pedals and casting anxious looks back at him.

Every time she did, he pretended he was working really hard to catch her.

Back at the cottage, she told him she had a wiener roast planned for dinner.

"Uh-uh," he said. "It's my turn. I'm planning dinner. And I'll give you a hint. I've had about all I can handle of budget-friendly for one day."

"But didn't you have fun?" she asked, a bit anxiously.

"I did have fun. Now it's my turn to show you some fun. And I just want to see you wear the nicest thing you own."

Her mouth moved. She was going to protest. But in the end, he could see intrigue won out.

Somewhere along the way they had thrown caution to the wind. They were exploring each other's worlds, trading places, and they were doing it with all the fascination and openness of exploring a foreign country.

A voice inside him tried to be heard.

It said, *Slow down. Be careful.* But it seemed the brakes on the bike weren't the only ones not working today.

CHAPTER SIXTEEN

ALLIE STOOD IN front of her mirror. The nicest thing she owned was a dress she had tried on only once, and thought she would never wear again.

It was the one she was supposed to wear for the *American Singing Star* finale. Almost every single outfit she had worn for that show had made her uncomfortable. At first the outfits had been too geeky: buttoned-to-the-top blouses and calf-length skirts. Then the metamorphosis had begun, but again Allie had been dressed as a character, not as herself.

And so she had worn too-tight black leather pantsuits, form-fitting tube dresses, one-piece short suits that lived up to the word *short*.

But when she had been presented with this dress and tried it on, it felt as if her heart had stopped.

It wasn't like anything she had ever worn, on the show or off. And it didn't really speak to who she was or to who the show had made her into.

The dress spoke to who Allie could be.

The famous designer Iggy had made it, and adjusted it just for her. The dress was two things: it was the sea and it was flame. The top of it was the color of fire, reds and oranges and yellows licking together. Those colors poured down the dress like the slow ooze of lava, and then exploded into the turquoises and navy blues of molten rock hitting the sea.

It had a low V in the front, another at the back, a belt at the tininess of her waist. And then the dress swept down, past her knees, her calves exposed in a swirl of gauzy sea foam fabric.

When Allie had missed the finale, nobody had asked her for the dress back. They hadn't asked her for the shoes, or even the jewelry that came with it. She wasn't sure if it was an oversight, a payment or an apology.

Naturally, given the disastrous circumstances her claim to fame had ended with, she had sworn she would never wear the dress.

Now she was glad for that. She was glad the public had never seen her in it. And she was glad Ryan had never seen her in it.

She contemplated how she could think his name with absolutely no emotional charge. If she felt anything at all, it was a strange pity, as if every single contestant on that ridiculous show had been caught in webs woven out of their own dreams.

The dress was not the dress of someone who had given up on dreams. It was the dress of someone who *owned* them, who knew exactly who they were, and were not the least bit afraid to show it.

When had she become that person?

Almost the instant she had let an intruder into her house, almost the instant she had said yes to the adventure of letting the strangers who knocked on her door—or broke it down, as the case may be—into her world.

She was seeing herself differently.

She was seeing herself like this. She had promised Sam they would do grown-up things, and she had somehow transformed, maybe for the first time in her life, into a complete grown-up.

Allie liked it. She looked sensual rather than sexy, mysterious rather than an open book. She looked like a woman who was passionate and complicated and confident. She twirled in the mirror. She flicked her hair. She wished for just one change to those horrid black tips...but to-night, she did not cover it.

She strapped on the tiny shoes with their impossible heels. She felt grateful for all the hours practicing moves on heels for the show. Thanks to dozens of rehearsals, she could practically turn a cartwheel in high heels.

She took the necklace that had come with the ensemble. The necklace flashed and reflected the flames of the dress. It looked like diamonds though, of course, it was fake, like everything on that show had been fake.

They had tried to make her into a fake.

She gave the exhausted Popsy, stretched out full length on her bed, a pat on the head and a scratch on the tummy. Then she took a deep breath and stepped out her bedroom door. She went down the hall and into the kitchen.

Sam sat at the table. He was looking at his phone, and so engrossed in whatever he was seeing that he didn't look up.

It gave Allie a moment to study him. He wasn't as dressed up as her. Obviously his best suit had not come on beach holiday with him. Still, Sam was looking pretty glorious himself.

Dressed in jeans, the dark navy of brand-new denim and a pressed shirt, he looked strong and lean and confident. He was freshly shaven, his hair combed, but his clothes and his grooming only added to his allure, because what he was, he carried inside himself.

For a moment, she felt almost intimidated

by the aura of power and control around him, but then he noticed her and, with a grin that made him *her* Sam again, he turned the screen toward her. A video was playing, Cody in the foreground dancing happily in front of the tiger enclosure.

His grin faded as he took her in. The phone dropped from his hand. His mouth opened and then closed again.

In his eyes, she saw the reflection of what she was.

And for the first time, Allie stood in the full glory and gratitude of the fact that *American Singing Star* had not succeeded in making her into what they wanted her to be.

He got up from the table and came and took her shoulders in his hands.

"How can you look so dressed up without a suit?" she asked, looking up into his face, into the desire-darkened color of his familiar brown eyes.

He was a man comfortable in T-shirts and shorts and pajama bottoms and flip-flops. But he was also powerful and successful, rich beyond anything she had ever dreamed.

But she knew she had the confidence to explore this side of him, too. She was aware *her* Sam, the one who tossed Cody in the air, and left books open on their spines, and built sandcastles, and dove into the sea, and fixed things that needed to be fixed, was right here, coexisting with this man.

She was aware she wanted to know all of him.

She slipped her arm though his proffered elbow and he escorted her out to the car. The car was gorgeous, all deep leather and luxury.

But a faint smell clung to it, that made her laugh out loud.

They didn't drive very far. He went to the other side of Sugar Cone and pulled into the marina.

"You rented a boat?" she said. She felt her first moment of uncertainty. She wasn't dressed for a boat. What if his idea of showing her his world involved baiting hooks? No, Sam simply wasn't the kind of guy who would get something like that so wrong. You did not tell a woman to wear her best and take her fishing.

"Not exactly a boat," he said. "Not like a rubber dingy or a fishing boat. Actually, not even like a motor boat." He pulled up at a slip.

Her mouth fell open.

Behind an arch and beyond a gangplank, a boat bobbed graciously. Or would this be called a boat?

A yacht was probably the correct term.

While she sat there, stunned, a uniformed

man came and opened her door, saluted them both as Sam took her arm and they made their way up the slightly swaying gangplank. Another uniformed man waited at the top.

"Mr. Walker, Ms. Cook, welcome abroad the *Queen of Love*."

Allie gasped at the name.

"I'm Clark and I'll be your steward for your time with us. We're about to set sail, so I'll get you settled with a drink and then if you want a tour of the yacht I'd be happy to give it to you *or* I can take you straight to the dining area."

"A drink would be nice," Sam decided for them, thank goodness, since it felt as if the cat had her tongue.

They were brought to a fabulous area in the bow of the boat, a semi-circle of deep white leather furniture.

Champagne was presented in flutes, and a plate of hors d'oeuvres was set out.

Clark went to attend to whatever yacht people attended to while a boat set sail, and then returned.

"May I show you the boat?" he asked. He took them through a main door and Allie stopped. It was a beautiful living room, more white leather, with a white grand piano to one side and a completely stocked bar on the other.

"We're supposed to have clear sailing for

your dinner cruise tonight, however, if you are more comfortable in here, please just let me know."

They followed him through the yacht, being introduced to any crew they came across and finally ending in the wheel house where they met the captain. Allie noticed Sam was watching her with a smile as one experience after another unfolded in front of her.

"Just own it," he told her quietly.

"But what does—"

She stopped herself. Did it matter what it cost? He could obviously afford it, and he wanted to give it to her. And so she surrendered to it, she just gave herself over to the complete enjoyment of this exquisite experience Sam was giving her.

Was it a date? If the movie, yoga on the beach and getting sweaty riding bicycles had left any doubt, this did not.

They went out to sea, and anchored off a lovely little island. It had a cottage on it that reminded her of her house. They were given the choice of the outdoor or indoor dining room. Sam wanted her to choose, and she chose the outdoor dining room.

On the port side, the cottage lights came on and splashed across the sea, and on the starboard side, way in the distance, they could see as the lights of Sugar Cone Beach winked on, and the ones in the hills above it. The sea became like a dark piece of velvet studded with the jewels of reflected light.

Dinner was served.

"And I thought the restaurant last night was swanky," Allie managed, as dish after dish of exquisite food was presented to them under inky dark skies, by staff who were so graceful and quiet, it was almost as though they were alone.

The meal finished and coffee came.

And then the lights were lowered, and music poured through speakers.

"Would you care to dance?" Sam asked her.

She closed her eyes, as the dreamlike quality of the evening intensified. Then she opened them, looked at him and nodded. She put her hand in his. In a moment, her forehead resting on his chest, his chin on the top of her heard, they swayed together, letting all the magic they were experiencing outside of themselves come in.

Was it just days ago, Allie wondered dreamily, that she had thought she knew what a perfect moment was?

The truth was she had no idea.

And for the first time in a long, long time, she trusted it.

She looked up into his face. His eyes were closed and he was without a doubt the most beautiful human being she had ever seen. She nestled deeper into his chest, and put her arms around him, pressing into the small of his back to bring him closer to her.

She thought back over their days together.

He wasn't just beautiful outside. He was beautiful inside, too.

"I'll remember this moment forever," she whispered to him. And for an instant, it pierced the perfection of the moment, a reminder that all good things ended.

They could not dance on this deck forever.

Sam and Cody would be leaving soon. And they had never once discussed what happened next.

But in this perfect moment, it felt as if Allie knew exactly what happened next.

What they had experienced between them over the past few days was too strong to just walk away from.

This was the beginning of the courtship. Not the end.

She reached up, and took his lips with hers.

Sam tasted of champagne and the night stars. He tasted of the sea and of every great mystery humans had ever explored together. He tasted of gentleness and he tasted of strength. He tasted of simplicity and he tasted of complexity.

Allie shivered under the taste of his lips, the red-hot touch of his hand on the nakedness of her back, the way he pulled her into him, both savage and sensitive.

The kiss validated all she knew and all she was feeling.

And she tasted the beauty of him so fully that something in her that had been unfinished was suddenly completed.

Until he pulled away from her, stepped back, raked a hand through the dark crispness of his hair.

"I'm not sure we should go there," he whispered huskily. "I'm not sure."

How was that possible? How could he be not sure, when she had never been more certain of anything in her whole life?

That's what you get, a little voice inside chided her, *for having faith in perfect moments. Again.*

CHAPTER SEVENTEEN

THEY DROVE HOME in silence, some tension in the air between them that he wanted to move away from, and that Allie wanted to move toward.

"I'm not ready to go to bed," Allie said when they arrived at the cottage and went in the door.

"You're exhausting me," Sam informed her. "Don't you ever sleep?"

But she glanced at Sam from under her eyelashes, and he did not look exhausted.

They were home from their magical evening, at that awkward moment when it was time to say good-night, go to their separate rooms and shut the doors.

Lie awake and listen to each other breathing.

"I'm not ready for bed," she said, again.

He sighed. "Me, either. You know what I want?"

Oh, yeah, she knew what he wanted. She had seen it in his eyes tonight when they had danced, felt it in the heat of his body when the music had turned slow.

"What do you want?" Allie whispered.

He leaned forward. She thought he was going to kiss her. But he didn't. He touched her hair.

"I want to cut this."

"What?"

"I want to get rid of those little black tips. I want to banish Tempest forever."

Hmm…interesting…just when she wanted to let Tempest out.

Without waiting for her answer, he led her out onto the deck. He placed a stool in the center of it, and beckoned for her to sit down.

He went back into the house and got a towel and a clothespin, and secured them around her neck.

"It feels like Superman's cape," she said softly.

"Maybe that's what it is when you become yourself."

And then with exquisite tenderness he began to cut her hair. Deliberately, his hands brushed the soft nape of her neck. Deliberately, he placed his lips where his fingertips had been. The black hair fell around her, bit by bit, and his lips and hands took the place of everything that hair had represented.

"It's kind of like Sampson and Delilah," she told him softly, "only in reverse. My strength is coming back to me with every snip. I am becoming more who I am, not less."

Finally, he was finished. He took off the towel and stood back regarding her. He took his fingers and ran them through her hair. He fluffed it. He acted as though he could not get enough of staring at her.

"And who are you?" he asked.

"It's my turn to pick what we do. I want to swim with you," she said, and heard the huskiness in her voice. "I want to skinny-dip with you in the ocean."

"That's not a good idea," he said.

"I think it is," she decided. "I'm all done with letting other people decide what the good ideas are, even you."

Even you.

As if he mattered to her, but not as much as she mattered to herself. Allie had been beautiful before. As she interacted with him, and Cody and her guitar. But Allie stepping out of that pile of dark hair and fully into herself was more than beautiful.

It was irresistible.

She went into the house, and came back out with a towel wrapped around her.

Sam could feel his mouth going dry. She was naked under that towel.

He tried to reason with himself: she was *always* naked under something, her clothes, her bathing suit.

She walked by him, and helplessly he followed her to the water's edge.

She dropped the towel, and stood there. The night was dark and yet her skin glowed white, luminescent. She gave him one look, one seductive smile, and dove into the waves.

He dropped his shorts and followed her into the water.

She was swimming out beyond the break, treading water and tilting her head to the stars.

"You're going to get us arrested," he told her huskily.

She turned her face away from the stars and looked at him. He saw her bravery. He saw what she was asking.

He did what he had wanted to do since they had danced together, since he had cut her hair.

Since the first time he had tasted her lips, probably since the first time he had seen her, lying on the floor, those huge eyes taking him in.

Even then, the bravery had been there.

He closed the small distance of dark water between them. He growled her name. She answered by twining her arms around his neck, by pressing herself against him. Her skin was hot in contrast to the cool of the water. Her body was substance, something you could hang onto, something solid in a liquid world.

He took her lips.

Her answer was tentative. A tasting. A nibble.

And then less tentative. Her hands twined more tightly around him, and her mouth invited him deeper.

He could not refuse the invitation. He was a man who had been dying of hunger and thirst, and this moment offered him what he had turned his back on.

Life.

Her lips tasted of seawater and hope. Her lips tasted of the wine she had sipped earlier and of dreams. Her lips tasted of laughter.

Her lips tasted of a future.

He groaned, and pulled her to him. He carried her out of the water.

She nestled into him. "Warrior," she said, the maiden being carried off.

But nothing could be further from the truth. He was not a warrior—he was the conquered. This was the very thing he was sworn to fight.

But his weakness was such that he could not remember why he needed to fight. He set her down slowly, pulled on his shorts, watched out of the corner of his eye as she pulled the towel around herself.

And then he scooped her back up. He carried her through the darkness, through the sand, aware she felt featherlight. How could someone so powerful be so light?

He slid open the patio screen with his foot, carried her through the darkened house and to his bedroom. He tossed her on the bed, and stood drinking her in, the unearthly beauty of her.

He laid down on the bed beside her. He traced the sacred places of her. He made her quiver with wanting him. He made her sigh and cry. He made her play out each of the things going on inside of him.

Far away, something was trying to pierce his awareness.

"Leave it," she whispered, a plea.

But he pushed up on his elbows and listened. It was his phone, in some faraway room.

Boing. Boing. Boing.

Allie's brow furrowed as she recognized the tone. "That's Kathy and Bill's ring tone," she said, sudden panic, that mirrored his own, in her voice.

"What time is it?" she asked.

He looked at the clock beside her bed. It was

nearly three in the morning. Nothing good had ever come from a three-in-the-morning phone call.

He got up and raced through the house, following the sound of the phone. Allie, the towel pulled around her, was right behind him. The phone had been abandoned out on the deck.

He found it, and stabbed at the keypad in the darkness.

"Hello?" he cried desperately.

He could hear a sound, but not a voice. He was pretty sure it was Kathy, but she wasn't speaking.

She was crying.

It was a terrifying reminder of what happened when you let go of control, what happened when you let your guard down.

"What's happened?" Sam demanded. "What's happened to Cody?"

"Nothing," Kathy managed to stammer. "Sam, he's fine. I'm sorry I frightened you. No, he's more than fine. He's already gone back to sleep. But I wanted you to know.

"He spoke."

Sam knew he should ask questions. A good person would ask questions. A good person would not make it all about him. A good person would at least ask what Cody said.

He was silent, because he could not trust his voice if he spoke.

Kathy laughed, a little nervously. "I'm sorry. It's the middle of the night. I probably shouldn't have woken you. But Cody woke up, and he spoke, and I just wanted you to know so badly."

"Thank you," he said, forcing the words out past the lump in his throat. He could not trust himself to say more.

"I'll let you go." She was crying again. "I just wanted you to know. We're going to leave really early. We'll be back at the beach house in the morning. Come for breakfast. You and Allie. I'll tell you all about it then."

Allie was at his side as he ended the call, looking at him with those huge eyes.

"Is everything okay? Is Cody okay?"

"Yeah," he said, "everything is fine."

"Sam?"

Allie was touching him. Her hand on his naked skin felt scorching, like a brand. She was gazing at him with a look that could steal whatever was left of his strength.

But life had just reminded him of the danger of the kind of moments—minutes, hours, days—that he had let himself share with her.

Just as he relaxed, just as he began to allow himself to have hope, life let you know.

You are a failure.

Not at business. When it came to business, he had the proverbial Midas touch. But where it really mattered? With people?

He had failed his nephew. A few days with other people—normal people, wholesome people—and Cody had spoken.

But his failures had begun long before that. He had failed his sister and brother-in-law. He had failed at marriage.

And he would fail Allie, too.

He knew what he needed to do. And he knew it was going to be the hardest thing he had ever done.

"What is going on?" Allie demanded. "What's happened to Cody?"

He forced his mouth into a smile. He forced himself not to look at her mouth, or her hair still wet from the sea, with no black left in it. He forced himself not to look at the long stretches of her not covered in the towel.

"Cody spoke," he said. "Kathy wanted to let me know."

"What did he say?" she asked. Her eyes filled with tears, joyous tears. "Sam! This is incredible."

She didn't get it. At all.

He had come here looking for an answer, looking for a sure direction, needing to know what was best for Cody.

He had come here begging to know what was right.

And now he knew.

"You," he said, "should not be luring men you barely know into middle-of-the-night naked swims with you."

"Barely know?" she whispered.

"No pun intended," he said coldly, and was satisfied to see her flinch and pull that towel a little tighter around her body.

It would make it easier for her if the cut was cruel. Oh, who was he kidding? It would make it easier for him if she didn't know the truth.

If she knew the truth—how hard it was to walk away from the light and back into darkness—she might wrap her arms around him again. She might soothe the demons in him with the sound of her voice. She might sing him back to *this* world.

He couldn't drag her down with him. He despised himself for how badly he wanted to go back into the circle of her arms, the comfort she was promising him.

He'd almost taken advantage of this fragile, broken girl.

Oh, sure he had cut her hair, he had led her part way back to who he could see she was. But would there be a worse choice than him to restore her?

No, he would be the worst choice.

He went into his bedroom. He shut the door, not with a slam, that might have revealed way too much, but with a click that said nothing at all.

He laid down in the bed they had shared. He could taste her on the air, and smell her in his sheets.

He waited until he heard her go to bed. And then he waited an hour beyond that. The dawn was coming up when he tiptoed out the door, a carelessly packed bag over his shoulder, and left.

He left Popsy with her. Even the dog knew the truth about him.

Allie woke up in the morning, with Popsy licking her face frantically. She realized it was very late. Well, it had been very late when she had finally slept.

At first the dog's attention made her feel happy, but then memories of the night before crept in. She remembered the terrible coldness in Sam's face after that phone call, and how nasty he had been to her. Then she became aware of a silence in the cottage, a feeling of utter emptiness.

She got up and raced to Sam's room. The bed was neatly made. The closet was empty. She ran to the front room and looked out the window. His car was gone.

She went to Cody's room. His things were still there, his books, his suitcase. Sam would not abandon Cody.

Or Popsy.

With panic rising in her, she ran all the way down the beach to Kathy and Bill's. It looked as if they had just gotten back. Kathy opened the door, and let her in.

"Is Sam here?"

"Here? No. Why would he—"

"I woke up this morning, and he was gone." She tried to keep the panic out of her voice. She couldn't let Cody hear. "Something happened last night when you called. I don't know what—"

Kathy's phone rang. She looked at it, and then nodded at Allie. "Sam? Allie's here. Where are you?"

She listened and then said, "Sam, you've got this all wrong. When Cody woke up he said—"

She frowned and stared at her phone. "He's hung up on me."

"What did he say?" Allie breathed.

"Cody said *Need Unca.*"

As important as it was for Allie to hear that, that wasn't what she meant. "What did Sam say?"

Kathy shot a look toward the hallway to make sure no little ears listened. "Something about meeting with his lawyers. Something about us, Bill and I, taking custody of Cody."

Allie felt as if she was breaking apart inside. "He was worried from the moment he arrived that that's what you wanted."

"What? We never wanted that. Of course we love Cody. Of course we are aware that Cody is how Adam goes on. We have been exploring how to spend more time with him. Bill has been looking at a transfer to his company's American office. That's part of the reason for this trip. We feel Sam is as much a part of our family as Cody is. It's so apparent how they have gotten each other through this. We can see the bond. Anyone could see the bond. How could he think we would want to break that bond?"

"He thought Adam and Sue probably named him guardian as a lark, back when they thought nothing bad could ever happen to them."

"You know, nobody liked a lark as much as Adam. And Sue, too. But when it came to their child? That's the most ridiculous thing I ever heard. They would have made that decision with all the weight it needed. And they made the right one. It's so obvious when you see Sam with Cody, don't you think?"

"Cody talked for you, not him. Sam will see

that as a failure, as proof that he's not the best person for Cody."

Kathy was watching her intently. Somehow, as she looked at Allie, the worry lines faded from her face.

"Oh, my," she said. "It's all way more complicated than Sam and Cody, isn't it?"

"In what way?" Allie stammered.

"You love him. And I wonder how he feels about you."

CHAPTER EIGHTEEN

"L-LOVE HIM?" ALLIE STAMMERED. "That's impossible."

She thought of Sam's final words to her, about luring men she barely knew into naked middle-of-the-night swims with her.

"And he doesn't have feelings for me. Or at least not positive ones."

But even as she told herself it was impossible, even as she told herself Sam did not have feelings for her, her heart was singing a different tune entirely. Kathy was smiling at her.

"I barely know him," Allie said, and then realized she had parroted the hurtful words he had said to her last night.

"You know, the very first time I laid eyes on Bill, something in me sighed, and said, *That's him.*"

"Well, I had that experience, too, only it wasn't with Sam, and the guy I had it with definitely wasn't *him.* I don't believe in fairy tales."

"Don't you? Don't you ever ask yourself what fairy tales are based on, and why they have survived the test of time? Other stories come and they go. But those ones—those stories of love winning out over all the obstacles put in its way—they stay, don't they? Generation after generation, drawn to them, finding comfort in them."

"I don't know what to do," Allie whispered.

"Of course you do," Kathy said. "Your heart knows exactly what to do."

And Allie realized Kathy was right.

On two counts. Allie had fallen in love with Sam. And she knew you did not love someone and allow them to carry that enormous burden of pain by themselves. She saw his hurtful words last night for what they were, an attempt to keep what was going on between them at bay, a fear of hope.

"I don't even know where he lives," she whispered.

"I do," Kathy said. "I do."

He lived a long way away. Far enough away that some of the confidence and certainty that Kathy had made her feel, that she had felt as she looked in the mirror at her freshly snipped hair, had abandoned her.

The confidence faded yet again when she parked in front of Sam Walker's apartment building. The building reminded her what the past days had helped her forget. They were from totally different worlds.

She had known that from the beginning. She had told him that, for Pete's sake. That they were an impossible match.

The building was gorgeous: stone and glass and steel. There was going to be a guard at the door, and he was not going to let her in.

But for some reason Kathy's words gave her courage.

There was a reason fairy tales survived. Obstacles could be overcome. There could be happily ever after.

This, she reminded herself sternly, was not about her. It wasn't just Kathy giving her courage. It was the legacy of Allie's grandmother. Nobody had championed love more than her grandmother.

She had a sudden thought: all those beautiful weeks with Gram, after Ryan's betrayal and the collapse of her dreams, before her grandmother had died. They had discussed the cottage going to Allie, but her grandmother had never once mentioned Sam's contract or his family, even though they had obviously been a part of her life for a long time. Was it possible her Gram had hoped a chance meeting between Allie and Sam could bring this outcome? Love?

It made Allie feel both happy and strong to think of her grandmother sweetly, and a little sneakily, trying to engineer her happiness as her last gift to her.

Now she felt tuned in to love and she listened. Love told Allie not to make it about herself. It was about him. It was about going in after him, when he thought he knew what was best for everyone.

She got out of her car. It seemed like the wrong kind of car to be parked in front of a building like this.

The doorman seemed to think so, too. He actually frowned as he held open the door for her.

While she'd been on *American Singing Star* she'd been exposed to many places like this: oozing the wealth of people who had arrived. Water trickled down a stone wall behind the desk and into a pond. The lobby had two deep leather couches facing each other in front of a fireplace. One of them looked as if it could be worth quite a bit more than her car.

Being in this kind of place when she was on the show had always made her feel *less than*, always made her feel like an imposter. It made her feel as if it was just a matter of time before they discovered who she really was and tossed her out.

But she didn't feel any of those things this time.

She found herself thinking: *This beautiful glass box is where he thinks he belongs?*

She could feel her resolve returning as she marched up to the desk. The security person looked intimidating, military bearing, probably a former Navy SEAL or something equally immovable. He was wearing a name tag that said *Benson*.

"I'm going up to see Sam Walker," she said. "I don't want to be announced."

His jaw dropped. "Uh, that's not exactly how it works."

"It's life-or-death," she said firmly.

The guy cocked his head at her, skeptically, and then his brows lifted. "Hey, aren't you Tempest?"

She waited for the look that followed, the judgment, the scorn.

It didn't come. Instead, the man's expression softened. "They sure threw you under the bus, didn't they?"

She knew she had stumbled upon a true fan. She knew if she said she was Tempest, the door would be opened for her. But she didn't want the door—especially not this door to Sam—opened for that reason.

Allie realized just a short time ago, she would have whole-heartedly agreed with him.

"Mr. Benson," she said, and heard the

strength in her words, "I am not Tempest, and I never was. I was not thrown under the bus, I walked in front of it, with my eyes wide open. It was extraordinarily painful, but if it took a few obstacles for me to arrive at the conclusion that each of my choices has led me to exactly where I am today, every one of those obstacles was worth it."

His whole face opened up, a man who knew a few things—didn't everyone in the human family?—about obstacles.

"I'm Allie," she said. "Allie Cook. And I'm here to see Sam Walker on a matter of the heart."

"Just Benson," he said. "No Mister. I'll take you up, you need an elevator key to open at his floor."

His floor? Now was not the time to be weak. "Thank you," she said. When Benson got up from behind his desk, she noticed he really did know a thing or two about obstacles. He only had one leg.

"He got what he deserved, anyway, our boy Ryan."

"What do you mean?"

He squinted at her. "You don't know?"

"I turned my back on all of it when it ended." Turned her back wasn't exactly accurate. She had dug a hole. And she would still be in it, if it weren't for Sam.

"Smart to not look back. I saw it about Ryan in the tabloids. It wasn't even a headline. That's the thing about those talent shows, isn't it? You never hear what happens to any of those people next. Even the winners seem to fade away like cheap ink on advertising flyers. His record deal fell through. He's singing on cruise ships."

Strangely, that was the exact moment Allie knew just how much she had come to love Sam Walker.

Because a heart that held love could have no room for any malice toward another human being.

She didn't know she had been hanging on to anything, until that moment before the elevator doors whispered open, and she forgave Ryan.

And it made her feel strong, and absolutely ready for what she had to do next.

The feeling of strength lasted two seconds. The absolute opulence of the apartment beyond the opened elevator door hit her like a brick.

She considered telling Benson to close the door and take her back down. But he was looking at her, like a man who knew a thing or two about courage, and as if he had an expectation of her.

And then Allie realized that *this* was the perfect moment she had always longed for. It was the moment love called her, and asked her to be bigger than herself, and more courageous than she had ever been. Hadn't she started to recognize what love required that day she had come down from the hills to be with Sam, instead of hiding?

In this moment, she recognized exactly what love did. It was a kind of suspension of self, that asked not *what do* I *need*? but *what does* he *need*?

She stepped out of the elevator, and the door whispered shut behind her, taking away her escape route.

The far wall of the apartment was probably all windows, though you couldn't tell that at the moment, because the curtains were all drawn and it had the ambience of a cave.

She heard a growl.

And a bear's cave at that.

"Sam?" Her eyes adjusted to the dark. He was sitting up on a sofa, glaring at her, but he was rumpled looking, and she knew he had slept there.

In the course of just a few hours, he had changed completely. His hair was sticking up all over the place, his face was shadowed with whiskers, his T-shirt had a stain on the front.

He was in boxer shorts. He looked haggard. And he looked tormented.

"What do you want?" he snapped.

"I want to know why you left."

He snorted. "I think that's obvious."

"It's not to me. You'll have to explain it."

She held her breath. He looked like he was in a dangerous and foul mood, the kind of mood that told nosy people to get lost, to leave him alone.

But, instead of telling her to get lost, to go away, Sam took a shaky breath, and Allie felt herself start breathing again.

"I'm a failure, Allie. Do you get that?"

"I'm afraid I don't. Looking around it seems as if you are the furthest thing from a failure."

He snorted. "You, of all people, know that none of this matters."

"That's true."

"What matters is being there for people when they need you. Knowing the right thing to do. Cody needs a family, not some bumbling uncle. That's why he finally talked. You know it is. Because they knew how to make him happy. And I didn't."

"You never asked what he said," she told him softly. "When he spoke."

"It doesn't matter. He spoke. He spoke when he was with them and he never did it for me."

"The words he said were *Need Unca.*"

Sam went very still. He rubbed his eyes. She thought she saw a tremble in his shoulders.

"A three-year-old doesn't know what he needs. I just had a video chat with him. He was fine. Happy. Learning to make blueberry pancakes. Not that *he* chatted. Nope. Silence for me. I've failed him. I told you about my first wife, I failed her, too.

"This is the part you don't know, Allie, that you really, really need to know. I failed Adam and Sue. After my parents died, I promised myself I would look after her, that I would never let anything bad happen to her again."

The pain was quivering in the air around him. His voice was a croak of pure, unadulterated feeling.

"I was supposed to be with them that night. I begged off. You know why? Because some woman, named Bambi or Bobbi or Barbie, called and made me an offer I couldn't refuse. It was more important to me than them.

"If I had gone with them, maybe I would have been driving. Maybe we would have taken a different route, or left at a different time. Maybe it could have been me, instead of them."

He put his head in his hands.

Allie could not bear to not be with him. She went and sank on the couch beside him and put her hands on his shoulders.

She could feel the strength he could not feel. She could see the bravery he was blind to.

She could sense the torment that he was carrying alone, that he could not control the fates of those he loved, and she could not let him be alone with it anymore.

"At the very least, I could have had those moments with them," Sam said hoarsely. "One last night. To cherish them. To hold on to. Maybe I could have told Sue I loved her. I never said that to her. Thought it was sappy. Unmanly. Even after Mom and Dad died, I never said it. I never said it to him, either. I never told Adam I loved him like he was my brother.

"Love," he snorted. "I don't know anything about love. It's a relief that Cody is going to go with them, with Bill and Kathy. I have a life. I need my life back. My old life. Parties. Good times. Racking up successes like billiard balls before the break."

"Liar," she said, oh, so tenderly, just as he had called her a liar when she had claimed her independence and strength and resilience.

Now she could see the lie he was telling himself.

"The lie you are telling yourself," she said softly, "is that you are terrified of failure."

"That's not a lie."

"What you're really terrified of is love.

You're so afraid of it wounding you again. So afraid that all your strength will not be enough. Not just to save yourself. I don't even think you care about yourself. You're afraid all your strength won't be enough to save others."

He was silent, so silent.

"You are," she said softly, "sacrificing your own happiness to do what you think is right. For me. For Cody. For Bill. For Kathy. Ironically, isn't that love itself? The ability to put the needs of others ahead of your own?"

Silent.

"I need you," she whispered.

"No! You are better off without me. Don't you get it? Both of you. Cody and you—"

She stopped him with a raised hand. "Unfortunately for you, Sam, you've hit me at a point in my life where I'm not letting anyone else decide for me what I need. I need you. And you need me. Desperately."

"I don't need you," he said scornfully, "especially not desperately."

She smiled at him. She touched his cheek. She looked deep into his eyes. "Especially desperately," she told him.

And then, tenderly, she claimed his lips, and kissed him.

Desperately.

And he answered her with equal desperation.

* * *

A long time later, Sam broke away from her kiss. How was it that something rooted in complete desperation could make him feel as if he had been pulled back from the brink?

He was aware that everything he had learned as a lifeguard was wrong. Completely and totally wrong.

Because he was not pulling her down with him.

She had the lifesaving ring. It was called love.

And it was strong enough to hold them both. It was strong enough to save them both.

CHAPTER NINETEEN

ALLIE SAT ON her back porch and strummed her guitar. The beach in front of her was packed. This was the last day of the Labor Day long weekend. Tomorrow, the beach would be nearly empty and the children would all be back in school.

She gulped. One of the neighbors who had joined the impromptu Fourth of July party at Kathy and Bill's—that seemed a lifetime ago—was a teacher. She had found Allie and asked if she would consider singing a few songs at the first-day-back-to-school assembly.

We can pay you a little bit.

Tomorrow. How had it arrived so quickly?

Unlike trying to produce a jingle for Phil's Steakhouse, which she had finally given up on, her guitar *loved* this assignment. The songs flowed out of her and her guitar: beloved children's rhymes, traditional tunes, folk songs, melodies and lyrics she created herself.

Was it the assignment that the guitar was re-acting to, or was her guitar absorbing the love that shimmered in the air around Allie's life? Everything, including the music, seemed infused with light.

It had been the most blissful summer she had ever known. She and Sam had given themselves over to exploring what had leaped up so suddenly and so unexpectedly between them.

They had spent the summer going back and forth between each other's houses. At her house, they did yoga on the beach, and learned to paddleboard. They tried beach volleyball. They hiked in the hills that surrounded Sugar Cone Beach. They bought kayaks, and rode bikes and had sunset picnics. They played music and tried out recipes and danced on the back porch as the stars came out and the waves lapped at the shore.

At his house, they experimented with his expensive coffee machine and his state-of-the-art kitchen. They enjoyed his home theater, and the condo complex swimming pool. They went to five-star restaurants and attended live theater. They went dancing at exclusive clubs. He took her to the first Major League ball game she had ever been at. They swooped over twisting highways on his motorbike, her arms wrapped around the solidness of his waist, the wind playing with the tufts of her hair.

Kathy and Bill bought the beach house that Allie had run by—again, it seemed a lifetime ago—that had been up for sale.

Bill went home to tie up loose ends in Australia before transferring to the United States, but Kathy and the kids stayed for the summer.

And so, as well as exploring the amazing energy that sizzled in the air between them, Allie and Sam learned what it was to become a family.

They took all the kids to every Sunday matinee at the local theater. They built sandcastles and baked cookies. They made blanket forts on rainy days. They worked their way through the menu of the local ice cream store. They introduced Popsy to the new puppy that Kathy brought home for the kids to help them adjust to their new life.

Cody, Nicole and Bryan were a willing and enthusiastic audience as Allie tested every song she played and every song she wrote on them. Soon, all the neighborhood kids, new friends to the gang, seemed to be showing up for the little impromptu concerts that sprang up.

Allie had a sense that she and Sam looked after Kathy and she looked after them. Cody happily stayed with his cousins as the romance unfolded between Allie and Sam. Kathy cheerfully accommodated, and encouraged, Allie and Sam's growing need for adult time, alone time.

Cody spoke a little more every day, blossoming under the love that had taken so many different forms around him, the love that filled his life until it spilled over.

As she strummed her guitar, and thought about the wonderful summer she had experienced, and the new adventure she was going to have tomorrow, Allie heard a noise at the front door.

She smiled at the full-circle feeling of the moment, set down the guitar, got up and greeted Sam just as he came through the door.

How could her heart still pound like this every single time she saw him? He kissed her, his lips warm and familiar and lovely, and then held her back and looked at her. "Are you ready for tomorrow?"

"As ready as I've ever been for anything."

He smiled at her, that now familiar smile that made her world feel right and complete and as if she could do anything. Climb mountains, jump from airplanes.

Sing to three hundred small children.

"I've got a little surprise for you," he said.

This was what he was like. He loved surprising her. He seemed to have a theme, his gifts seemed intent on filling her world with beauty. They almost always had something to do with painting pictures, telling stories, or singing songs.

And so he had made her gifts of exquisite paintings and pieces of art, wonderful books, both old and new, and beautiful instruments like an antique ukulele.

Which she was going to use in one of her new songs tomorrow.

He handed her an envelope, and watched her intently as she opened it. She looked at the pieces of paper without comprehension.

"What is this?"

"Kathy has already agreed to babysit."

"Tickets?"

He nodded. "Airline tickets."

"To Paris," she whispered. Once, she realized, she had been afraid to go. Afraid of broken promises and her own expectations. Afraid to leave the safe little world she had created for herself.

But loving Sam had removed her limitations. It had filled her with curiosity about the world and a bold desire to explore it and to embrace all the adventures it held. Love had made her brave.

"It's supposed to be beautiful in the fall," he said, as if she needed coaxing.

"Are these first-class tickets?" she asked,

pretending disapproval. As she hoped, it got a rise out of him.

"Look, Allie, as much as every man wants to be loved for himself and not his money, I have long legs. I need to have more legroom. I know you'd be comfortable in one of the overhead bins, but, for once, can't you just go along?"

She gave up the charade of being disapproving, allowed herself a little shriek of pure delight and threw herself into his arms, covered his face with kisses. "Yes, yes and yes. I think it was Audrey Hepburn who said, 'Paris is always a good idea.'"

"You didn't think it was such a hot idea the first time I suggested it," he reminded her.

"You've been a good influence on me," she said, and fluttered her eyelashes at him demurely. He roared with the laughter that she loved drawing out of him.

Sam was quite familiar with Paris, but they explored it as if it was brand-new to both of them. They strolled the misty banks of the Seine at dawn, and experienced the Louvre at dusk. They ate take-away crepes, and freshly roasted chestnuts from street stalls. They drank *chocolat chaud* at the Café de Flore, one of the oldest cafés in Paris. A favorite historical haunt of painters, writers and philosophers—"The people who make the world beautiful," Sam reminded her—it served the melted chocolate and the hot milk in separate jugs. Then they walked the streets of St. Germaine until their feet hurt.

They reveled in the sights of Luxembourg Palace and its gorgeous gardens, kicking through piles of leaves with the delight of children. They discovered the underground world of the catacombs. They found the graves of Oscar Wilde and Jim Morrison in the Père Lachaise Cemetery.

Now, they sat in a small café with steamy windows, sampling the most delicious coffee and croissants Allie had ever tasted.

"This is the café you were going to recommend, when you first tried to get rid of me by sending me to Paris," she said softly, when they were settled.

Sam looked distracted. Normally he would have taken her words as an invitation to tease her about *Look what had happened because you didn't listen to me.*

"Is something wrong?" she asked him.

Sam looked flustered.

If there was one thing she had come to know about him, it was that he was never flustered. He handled life with great confidence and courage and aplomb.

They had just had a wonderful day, but he

did not seem to be filled with the kind of contentment or wonder such a day should bring.

Instead, Sam was patting his pockets and stammering.

"Have you lost your wallet?" she asked him.

"No, I—"

He found what he was looking for. He pulled back his chair and took a deep breath. He stood up.

And then he sank down on one knee if front of her. He held up a small box to her and snapped open the lid.

But it wasn't the light that shone from the ring that set her heart on fire. It was the light that shone from his eyes.

"Allie, I was wondering—"

He cleared his throat.

"Allie, I was thinking—"

She was crying so hard she couldn't help him out. The other patrons had stopped what they were doing. The waitstaff had stopped what they were doing.

The whole world stopped, even in this city that celebrated such things all the time, the whole world stopped in the absolute stillness of what was unfolding here.

The sacredness of it.

"Would you be my wife?" he whispered,

hoarsely. "Would you walk through this world, and the days of my life with me?"

His voice was gaining strength now.

"Would you be the one who gives me courage when mine falters, and who shows me the way home when I have become lost?"

Though not everyone in the restaurant understood English, everyone seemed to understand the universal language of the heart. There was not a sound: not a coffee cup rattled, not a teaspoon moved, not a throat was cleared.

"Would you allow me to be the one who helps you up when you stumble, and who shows you the way back to yourself when you forget who you are?

"Can I be the one who is there as you sing your songs to the world?"

Through the tears, she said yes. Through the tears she told him that every song was really for him.

That every song was really about love.

He came off his knee and stood above her. He held out his hand to her. She took it. And entered his embrace.

The café exploded into the sound of people cheering and clapping as Sam kissed Allie and Allie kissed Sam.

But neither of them could hear a single sound above the rapturous beating of their own hearts.

EPILOGUE

"Look," Cody called. "All you have to do,
Allie, is hold the kite. Throw it up in the air
when I tell you. Unca, you run!"

Cody was six. His three-year-old sturdiness
had given way to knobby knees and ribs that
showed, no matter how much they fed him.
Today, he was wearing a suit. It looked as if
he had already lost the bow tie, and the shirt
was rumpled where it was untucked from his
pants. Sam felt just a little gleeful about a six-
year-old's innate ability to thwart anyone's vi-
sion of perfection.

Sam did as he was told. He ran.

"Faster, Unca, faster."

Sam did not think he would ever stop mar-
veling at Cody's voice: strong, sure, light-filled.

"Okay, Allie, throw it!"

Sam turned to see the kite lift, then nose-
dive toward the earth. When he turned to
run again—hoping to make the kite catch the

wind—he lost his footing and fell headlong in the sand. He twisted into a roll, hoping Allie would admire his graceful athleticism. He turned to look at her, and felt the breath whoosh out of him more than it had when he fell.

Honestly? The baby was due any day. She should have looked like a leprechaun explosion in that tent of a jade green dress she was wearing. Instead, she looked gorgeous.

"I think you may have ruined the kite. You're definitely ruining your clothes!" she called to him, as if she hadn't noticed his brilliant recovery from his tumble at all.

Sam felt annoyed—again—at his mother-in-law. A beachfront wedding. So close to Allie's due date that she could have the baby out there on the beach. But there was no talking any sense to Professor Cook, Priscilla. She was bossy and controlling and easily the world's most annoying person. Sam was only sucking it up for Allie's sake.

He stopped his thoughts from going too far down that route, and gave himself over to the pureness of this moment, the joy shimmering in the air between the three of them, his family.

Three years.

Sam contemplated that, in the context of the brilliant light he felt he was standing in, despite the grayness of the day, despite Pricilla's aggravating wedding plans. He stood up and brushed off his pants, found the handle for the kite string as Cody and Allie fussed over the kite.

Time, he had heard over and over, *healed all wounds.*

This, he had found to be false. It was love, not time, that healed all wounds. Love, like the love he had experienced from his sister, Sue, and his friend and brother-in-law, Adam, making him ready when he had been blissfully unaware he would ever need readiness.

It was their love that had made him ready to say and do whatever love asked him to do.

The healing came from the love Allie gave him every day. And Cody.

Cody declared the kite flight worthy and ran toward him. "You have to run a little faster, Unca. Then it will go."

Sam looked back at the kite Allie was clutching, nearly said something and then didn't. Instead, with Cody trying breathlessly to keep up, he raced down the sand again.

Despite the fact they could have bought a dozen kites, or a hundred, or a thousand, Allie had insisted they make the kite themselves, following instructions they had found on the internet. Sam had carefully inspected their finished efforts last night. The kite was a thing of beauty, but the rainbow of colors on the hand-painted brown paper did not make it any more air-worthy. He had broken the truth to them as gently as he could. It would never fly.

And yet here he was running his heart out for it.

It was spring, the kind of blustery day that kept people off the beaches. It was a poor day for a beachfront wedding, and he could see, down the beach, the way he had come, the pagoda was already looking a bit bedraggled. He couldn't help but feel just a little happy about that.

For heaven's sake, it was a beach wedding. Why all the formality?

Beyond the pagoda was their Soul's Retreat. They had added the second floor to the cottage last year when they'd found out their news. It just wasn't going to be big enough for four of them as it was.

They'd renovated the first floor, too, taking down walls and adding windows, but somehow remaining faithful to the simplicity of the place, the soul of it.

Which was the love that lived there.

Still, the miracle of that love wasn't in the love he'd *received* in such generous abundance, both before and after the accident that had taken Sue and Adam—it was the love he had learned to *give.*

It was learning to be selfless in that giving—to put the needs of others ahead of his own, not resentfully and not reluctantly, but fully and generously—that had restored his heart.

He would do anything to have his sister back. And Adam.

And yet, sometimes, just for a second, when Cody tilted his head a certain way, there was Sue. And when he laughed, there was Adam. Going on.

So there was the basic truth: from Sam's darkest time had come his greatest lessons, from his darkest hours had come the reliance within himself that made him worthy of what Allie and Cody gave him every day.

And what Bill and Kathy, and Nicole and Bryan gave him. They would be here, soon, for the wedding, part of this crazy thing called family that Sam found himself totally immersed in.

What he and Allie's new baby would give him.

"How does it feel?" he had asked her the other night, his hand resting gently on the barrel-tightness of her tummy, the baby kicking furiously within.

"Like a miracle," she'd said.

"How does it feel that it's your own child?" he had asked softly.

She had stared at him, then blinked, as if the question was absurd. "They're all my children," she had said.

All her children.

The first Christmas they were together, she had made the kids of their family—Cody, Nicole and Bryan—a disc of all their favorite songs. And she had put in some of her own originals, including the never-before-heard "Pooperman's Cape."

When Bill had heard her music, he had sent it to his friend in Australia, the one who was a record producer.

Within a year, "Pooperman's Cape" was the number-one-selling children's song in Australia.

And then in Canada, and then and then and then…last year, she had made more money than him.

And yet she remained hilariously cheap. She *wanted* to make her own kites, and sew the new quilts for the beds.

Because she understood, perhaps better than most, it wasn't about the money.

Allie had found the part of herself that had been lost in that crazy world she had entered a long time ago. A world that had promised fame and fortune and acceptance, on the condition she sell her soul for it, on the condition she pretend to be someone and something that she was not.

They had all loved her—including her own mother—for someone she was not.

Some part of her had known the price was too high. Some part of her had retreated instead of moving forward.

But when she found herself, she was never letting go again of what she had found. That somehow the secret of life was not in having stuff—in fact, maybe all that stuff could overwhelm what was important—but in having moments. Experiences. Connections.

And she had connections. Now, they were *all* her children. The ones she visited in hospitals, the ones whose letters she always answered, the one out there flying the kite with her, the one she carried under her heart.

They were all her children.

And he had been given the amazing privilege of being there to watch her love unfold, of being the one who had helped her be brave enough. To see herself. To be herself.

Once, it seemed a long, long time ago, he had called her a liar when she had said she was strong. Independent. Self-reliant.

But then she had waded into the fire to get him. Was there really any strength, compared to that one? The absolute bravery of saying yes to what love asked of you?

She constantly taught him new things about love. She had asked Ryan, whose star had plummeted as quickly as it had risen, to be on one of the albums with her.

Sam had disagreed—vehemently—with that decision.

But she had explained to him, so patiently, that she and Ryan had both been so young, so easily manipulated by the promises of *American Singing Star*.

"They found what we both wanted most, and played it," she said. "He wanted recognition."

"And you?"

"I wanted love."

And now, finally, she had found it. And love had made her this: full and forgiving, able to share the bounty of it with others, even those Sam would have found unworthy. Ryan, who had thrown her under the bus, and Priscilla, who was not exactly a candidate for Mother of the Year.

According to Allie, love made you more than you were before, not less.

Other truths had come to him over these years, truths he might not have seen if tragedy did not backlight them.

Time was a gift that could never be taken lightly.

Love was a gift that could never be taken lightly.

They had learned, together, he and Allie, to treat those things with the awed reverence they deserved.

And they had learned, together, the most important lesson of all.

When love beckoned you, followed it.

Soon, Priscilla would arrive. And Allie's father, Jim, a quiet, retired professor and lover of music, just like Allie. He and her mother had reunited on social media a few months ago.

And even Priscilla seemed to know, finally, after a lifetime of the loneliness, of always being the one who was right, that when love beckoned, you followed it.

Priscilla and Jim were getting married on the beach today—rain or shine, Priscilla had proclaimed, and it looked like it would be rain—and settling here in California, so they could be near the grandkids.

Honestly, this messy thing called family gave Sam a headache sometimes. A headache, he realized, that he wouldn't trade for anything in the world.

"Now, Allie, throw it in the air now!"

Sam turned, breathless, just as Allie lifted

that rainbow-colored kite high, and then tossed it in the air.

And that kite, the one Sam told them would never fly, defied all the odds. Just as his own life had defied all the odds, that kite suddenly found the wind, and lifted and lifted and lifted.

Until it danced with heaven.

Cody and Allie shrieked their delight, clapped their hands, lifted their faces to the sky. The wind blew her long hair around her face.

"Oh!" Allie cried. "Oh, what a perfect moment!"

It was, Sam thought, letting his gaze drift back to the kite, tugging, yanking, pulling, like a wild horse that wanted to be free, as close to a perfect moment as any person could ever expect on this earth.

* * * * *

If you enjoyed this story,
check out these other great reads
from Cara Colter

Cinderella's Prince Under the Mistletoe
His Convenient Royal Bride
Snowbound with the Single Dad
Swept into the Tycoon's World

All available now!